2

THE GHOST
WHO
FELL IN LOVE

Other Dutton Books by Barbara Cartland

Love Locked In
The Wild, Unwilling Wife
The Passion and the Flower
Love, Lords, and Lady-Birds
The Chieftain Without a Heart
I Seek the Miraculous

Barbara Cartland

THE GHOST WHO FELL IN LOVE

E.P. DUTTON
New York

For information contact: E.P. Dutton, 2 Park Avenue, New York, N.Y. 10016

Library of Congress Cataloging in Publication Data

Cartland, Barbara, 1902-
    The ghost who fell in love.

    I. Title.
PZ3.C247Gh   1978   [PR6005.A765]   823'.9'12   77-28768

ISBN: 0-525-11350-9

Published simultaneously in Canada by Clarke, Irwin & Company Limited, Toronto and Vancouver

10 9 8 7 6 5 4 3 2 1

First Edition

Author's Note

The first race was run at Ascot on Saturday, August 11, 1711, under the patronage of Queen Anne. In this novel every description of Royal Ascot in 1822 is correct, including the race-horse owners, the jockeys, and the horses, with the exception of the winner of the Gold Cup. This was actually won by Sir Huldibrand, owned by Mr. Ramsbottom. Today the winner receives a Gold Cup, and twenty-five thousand pounds, which was added in 1975.

The very small enclosure round the Royal Stand, to which only those invited by George IV were admitted, was the beginning of the Royal Enclosure.

Up to the last war this was very exclusive and even today tickets are only obtainable from the Lord Chamberlain.

THE GHOST
WHO
FELL IN LOVE

Chapter One

"Demelza!"

Demelza raised her head from the book she was reading and listened.

"Demelza! Demelza!"

Hastily she jumped up and ran along the creaking boards of the Picture Gallery to the top of the stair

Below her in the hall was an extremely elegant figure, his handsome face upturned to hers, his head thrown back, his lips already forming her name again.

"Gerald!" she exclaimed. "I was not expecting you."

"I know you were not, Demmy," he said, using the childish nickname he had given her when he was only four years of age.

She ran down the stairs to throw her arms round her brother's neck.

"Careful!" he said warningly. "Mind my cravat!"

"A new style! Oh, Gerard, it is very smart!"

"That is what I thought," he said complacently. "It is called 'the Mathematical.' "

"It certainly looks difficult to achieve."

"It is!" he agreed. "It took me hours, and over a dozen muslins completely ruined."

"Let me look at you," Demelza said.

She stood back to admire the dashing figure he made in his tight champagne-coloured pantaloons, close-fitting cut-away coat, and elaborate waistcoat.

"Your new tailor does you proud!" she said at length, knowing he was waiting for her verdict. "But I am terrified at what the bill will be!"

"That is what I have come to talk to you about," Sir Gerard Langston replied.

Demelza gave a little cry.

"Gerard! . . . Not the duns?"

"It was almost as bad as that," her brother replied. "But let us talk about it in the Library. And I could do with a drink—the crowds on the roads were ghastly!"

"I can imagine that," Demelza said. "It is always the same before race-week."

The preparations for the Ascot Races always began well in advance of the meeting. The horses usually arrived first, to be installed in numerous stables round the course.

Visitors from the provinces set out on the long journey many days, even weeks, before the date fixed for the meeting, while from London people began to move into the neighbourhood of Ascot during the week before the races actually took place.

As they entered the Library, Gerard looked round him in a manner which surprised his sister, as if he were appraising the room.

Usually when he returned home it was either to collect his clothes which had been washed, ironed, and mended by her and their old Nurse, or else because his pockets were so empty that he had for the moment to give up his expensive lodgings in Half Moon Street.

"What are you looking for?" Demelza asked at last.

Gerard's eyes had wandered over the faded velvet curtains, the carpet, which was threadbare in places, and the arm-chairs, which had needed recovering for the last ten years.

Worn and shabby the room might be, but it still had a dignity and a beauty about it which made her brother say at length with almost a sigh of relief:

"It is not too bad, and after all only parvenues and the new rich have everything too slap-up and ship-shape."

"What are you talking about, dearest?" Demelza asked in her sweet voice.

"I have brought you some very exciting news," Gerard replied. "Hold your breath, because it will astonish you."

"What is it?" Demelza asked a little apprehensively.

"I have let the house for the whole of next week!"

There was a pause before Demelza said incredulously:

"Let the house? What can you . . . mean?"

"Exactly what I say," Gerard said, throwing himself down on the sofa, which creaked under his weight.

"But . . . why? What . . . for? To . . . whom?"

The questions tumbled from Demelza's lips and there was a marked silence before her brother answered:

"To the Earl of Trevarnon."

He saw Demelza's eyes widen and added quickly:

"Wait until you hear what he has offered me."

"But why should he want to come . . . here?"

"That is easy to answer," Gerard replied. "The Crown and Feathers at Bracknell was burnt down the night before last."

"Burnt down?" Demelza exclaimed. "How terrible! Was anybody hurt?"

"I have no idea," her brother replied carelessly, "but Trevarnon had taken the whole Inn for race-week."

"So now he has nowhere to go," Demelza said slowly.

"He was desperate," Gerard answered. "You know as well as I do that there is not a room, or even a bed, available in the whole district."

Demelza knew this was true.

Unlike the Epsom Races, which could be easily reached in a day from London, Ascot Race-course was nearly thirty miles from the Capital.

Only a few Corinthians drove there daily at a speed which necessitated a change of horses. For most race-goers it meant a five-day visit, which resulted in the whole neighbourhood being packed to bursting.

If, as she and her brother knew, one was fortunate enough to be a guest at Windsor Castle or at one of the country houses for which astronomical rents were paid, there were no problems.

But otherwise it meant being crammed into the extremely uncomfortable local Inns, which charged exorbitantly for the privilege. In some cases a guest returning from the Heath found he was expected to sleep on a sofa or even roll up on a hearth-rug.

Demelza could imagine, without her brother telling her, what a problem it would cause when one of the better Inns like the Crown and Feathers at Bracknell was burnt down on the Friday before race-week.

Gerard was telling her what had occurred.

"We were drinking in White's Club yesterday evening, when Trevarnon learnt the news, and asked: 'What the devil can I do?'

"No-one answered, and he went on:

" 'I have five horses entered for the meeting, one of them being Crusader! They are already on their way to Bracknell.' "

"Crusader?" Demelza repeated almost under her breath.

It was the horse she had been looking forward to seeing, for he had won a number of races already and every newspaper had published eulogies about his appearance and his pace.

"Exactly—Crusader!" her brother repeated. "And I stand to lose a packet if he does not run!"

"Oh, Gerard, how could you?" Demelza cried. "You know that you promised me you would not bet until you had paid off some of the bills you owe."

"But Crusader is a certainty!" Gerard answered. "The Earl himself has wagered a fortune on him."

"The Earl can afford to," Demelza said quietly.

"And so can I, now that I have let the house."

"You mean," Demelza asked, "That you are really allowing the Earl of Trevarnon and his party to come here?"

"That is what I am trying to tell you, Demmy," her brother replied. "Do not be a nit-wit about it! He is paying through the nose for the privilege, and God knows we need it!"

"How much?"

There was a little tremor in the words.

"One thousand guineas!"

There was an unmistakable note of elation in Gerard's voice, but his sister stared at him as if she could not have heard him aright.

"One thousand guineas?" she repeated after a moment. "It is . . . impossible! You cannot . . . mean it!"

"I tell you he was desperate," Gerard answered. "The Coffee-Room was crowded, and he looked round as if it had struck him that somebody present might have a house in the neighbourhood. Then his eyes fell on me.

" 'I seem to remember, Langston, that you live near Ascot,' he said slowly.

" 'That is true, My Lord,' I replied.

" 'And is your house fully occupied?'

" 'No, My Lord,' I answered, 'but I do not think it would be suitable for your requirements.'

" 'Anything with a roof would be suitable in the circumstances, and I presume you have stables?'

" 'Yes, there are stables,' I replied.

" 'For how many?' "

Gerard Langston threw out his hands.

"I told the truth, Demelza. What else could I do?"

"Go on with the story," his sister pleaded.

" 'About forty, My Lord,' I replied, and the Earl walked across the room and drew me aside.

" 'Have you any particular objection to me as a tenant?' he enquired.

" 'Certainly not, My Lord!'

" 'Then why so much hesitation?'

" 'The house is old, and, as I am seldom at home, there are few servants.'

" 'That is of little consequence,' the Earl replied. 'I will bring my own Chef, my Butler, and any number of footmen that are required.'

"I said nothing and after a moment he said:

" 'Would one thousand guineas be acceptable to you as rent for the week?' "

Gerard paused as if he was remembering how his own breath had been taken away at the magnificence of the sum. Then before his sister could speak he said:

"It is all settled, and he is arriving with his party tomorrow. The horses should be here later this evening."

"But, Gerard, how can we cope? There is only Nattie and old Betsy to do everything!"

"If he is uncomfortable the Earl has no-one to blame but himself," Gerard said airily. "And one thousand guineas, Demelza, think of it!"

He glanced at her a little uncomfortably as he said:

"I was just on the point of coming home and spending the rest of the summer here."

That meant, his sister knew, that he was completely broke.

No-one knew better than she did that it would have

been impossible for him to refuse such a generous offer, even though she could see innumerable difficulties ahead.

Langston Manor had been in the Langston family since the reign of Henry VIII and the dissolution of the Monasteries.

It had been added to and altered during the years, but it had kept its gabled roof, its twisting chimneys, its diamond-paned windows, and its air of mystery and other-worldliness, which Demelza attributed to the fact that it had originally housed dedicated Cistercian Monks.

The fortunes of the Langstons had fluctuated down the centuries: some members of the family had been immensely rich and Statesmen of great power and prestige, while others had been spend-thrifts who frittered away the family fortune.

Their father and grandfather both had belonged to the latter category, and Gerard in fact had inherited little but the house and a few acres of woodland.

He of course wished to live most of his time in London and associate with the Bucks and Beaux who had made themselves notorious during the Regency.

They were still the core of the sporting world which centred round the newly crowned King George IV.

If Gerard enjoyed himself in London, Demelza was forced to live very quietly at home.

She had never known any other life, so she did not miss the Society whirl to which she would have been entitled had her mother been alive and had there been any money.

She was in fact perfectly content helping their old Nurse keep the house in order, tending the garden, and spending much time reading.

Her real happiness was that she could ride her brother's horses, which, fortunately, he could not afford to stable in London.

He had one race-horse, Firebird, on which he built great hopes. He had left him to be trained by his sister and the old groom, Abbot, who had been at the Manor since they were children.

It was Abbot who had insisted they should enter Firebird in one race at Ascot, to be ridden by his grandson Jem Abbot.

Jem had grown up at the Manor and was just beginning to be noticed amongst the younger jockeys who looked for mounts at every well-known race-meeting.

It was from Jem that Demelza had heard of the unrivalled appearance and outstanding performances of Crusader, but it was from her brother that she had heard of the Earl of Trevarnon.

"All you have to do now," Gerard was saying, "is to leave things as tidy as you can, get in as much help as possible, and find somewhere to stay."

"F-find . . . somewhere to . . . stay?" Demelza repeated in astonishment.

"You can hardly remain here," he answered. "It is a bachelor-party, and anyway, as I have told you often enough, Trevarnon is a man's man. I admire him, but I certainly would not let him come in contact with my sister!"

"But . . . Gerard . . . where can I go?"

"There must be somewhere," he replied carelessly.

"But if I go away, it will be quite impossible for Nattie and Betsy to manage, and old Jacobs will forget to bring in the coal for the kitchen and clean the floors. He gets more senile every day."

"You cannot stay here, and that is the end of it!"

The way Gerard spoke told his sister that he was thinking of the Earl.

"Can he really be so wicked?" she asked.

There was no need for her to explain of whom she was speaking.

"He is the devil himself where women are con-

cerned," her brother replied. "I have never known a
man who can ride better, has more knowledge of
horses, is a finer shot, and is a sportsman in every possible way—except one."

"You have spoken of him before. I have often
thought he was not a . . . good companion for . . . you,"
Demelza said gently.

"Companion!" Gerard exclaimed. "I can hardly
aspire to that! He counts few people as his really intimate friends. He is pleasant to me, includes me in his
parties, and I admire him—of course I admire him. He
outshines every other Corinthian who was ever born,
but God, when it comes to women. . . !"

"He has never married?"

"He *is* married."

"I had no . . . idea. You have . . . never mentioned
. . . the Countess."

"She is mad—shut up in a mad-house, and has been
for the last twelve years."

"Mad! How terrible! You must feel very . . . sorry
for him."

"Sorry for Trevarnon?" Gerard laughed. "That is the
last thing anyone would be! He owns more property
than any other man in England and is as rich as
Croesus. They say he obliged the King when he was
Regent with enormous loans which will never be re-
paid."

"But for his wife to be . . . mad!"

"It does not seem to trouble him, but it is certainly
an obstacle to all the women who want to walk him
up the aisle."

"Perhaps he would like to be married."

"There is no chance of that as long as he has a wife
alive, and I assure you he turns to his advantage the
very fact that he is shackled."

Gerard laughed a little bitterly.

"If he leaves a woman weeping and broken-hearted,

she can hardly blame him when she knew from the
very beginning he could not marry her."

"I can understand . . . that," Demelza said.

"You understand nothing!" her brother snapped.
"And I am not having you coming into contact with
the Earl, and that is final! You will leave here this
evening, and with no more arguments about it."

"But where am I to go? I can hardly undertake the
journey to Northumberland to stay with Aunt Elizabeth
without anyone to accompany me, and if I take Nattie
with me I am sure Betsy will refuse to do anything!"

"Oh, God, you are making unnecessary difficulties!"
Gerard cried.

"I am not, I promise you I am not, dearest, but we
have to face facts. You know as well as I do that I
keep the house going, that I cook your meals when you
are here, that I see to the linen, the opening of the
rooms, and all the dusting."

"Then pay someone to do it while you are away!"
her brother replied in an exasperated tone.

"Pay whom?" Demelza asked. "Every available
woman on two legs is already engaged to wait on the
visitors to the races."

This was so irrefutably true that Gerard found there
was nothing he could say.

"And what is more," Demelza went on after a moment, "I cannot have strange servants spoiling the few
things we have left, like the sheets with real lace which
Mama always used and the pillow-cases she embroid-
ered so beautifully."

Her brother was about to speak, when she gave a little cry.

"I have thought of it! I know what I can do! I
have solved the whole . . . problem."

"Where are you going?"

"To the Priests'-Room!"

"To the Priests'-Room?" he echoed.

"I will sleep there," Demelza said. "No-one will know I am in the house, and when you are at the races I can tidy everything and put things ready for your return."

Gerard looked at her speculatively. Then he said slowly:

"I do not like it. It is too dangerous."

"Dangerous?" Demelza queried.

He was not prepared to explain, but it was as if he saw his sister in a different way for the first time.

He was so used to her that it had not struck him until now how exceedingly lovely she was, with a beauty that was different from that of the women he knew in London.

There was something very young and almost childlike in her small oval face and her huge eyes, which were the colour of a pansy.

It was a characteristic of the Langstons that their eyes looked purple in some lights.

Gerard followed the family tradition but, surprisingly, Demelza, while inheriting her father's eyes, had her mother's hair. It was such a pale gold that it sometimes appeared to be silver.

It was a strange combination, but at the same time it was so arresting and unusual that any man would be fascinated by it.

Demelza was four years younger than her brother, but Gerard thought of her as a child, except that in many ways she looked after him as if she were his mother.

Now he told himself that he had to protect her, especially from a man like the Earl of Trevarnon.

"Why are you staring at me?" Demelza asked.

He smiled and it made him look attractive and boyish.

"I was thinking that properly gowned you would be the toast of Saint James's."

"I hope not!" Demelza exclaimed. "Mama always said it was very . . . vulgar for ladies to be talked about in Clubs. In fact it meant they were not . . . ladies!"

"Well, you are not going to be, so the question does not arise," Gerard said with a sudden note of authority in his voice. "If I let you stay in the Priests'-Room, do you swear to me that you will not come out of the secret passages as long as Trevarnon or any of his guests is in the house?"

He paused before he added:

"I mean that, Demelza. You will give me your word of honour, or you and Nattie will have to go to Northumberland."

"Of course I promise you," Demelza said disarmingly. "You do not think I wish to meet men like the Earl or any of your other raffish friends? Although it fascinates me to hear you talking about them, I disapprove of most of them and all they do!"

Gerard laughed.

"Of which you know nothing, thank goodness! Well, I trust you. Perhaps I am doing the wrong thing, but I do understand that the whole household depends upon you."

"That is the nicest thing you have said to me," Demelza replied with a smile. "But, Gerard, as you are getting so much money, you will give me some for the wages and for our food when you are not here?"

"Yes, of course I will," her brother answered. "I am a cad to you in a lot of ways, Demelza, but just as you share the bad times, naturally you will share the good."

"Thank you, dearest, I knew you would understand, and I hate owing money to the local tradesmen."

She kissed her brother's cheek as she spoke and he said:

"I have not cashed Trevarnon's cheque yet, but here is a guinea or two to be going on with."

He drew some golden coins out of his pocket and put them into her hand, and Demelza kissed him again.

"Now I must go and get everything ready," she said. "There is very little time if the gentlemen are arriving tomorrow, and you had better go to the stables and tell Abbot to expect the horses. The stalls are all right except for the three at the end, where there are holes in the roof and the rain comes in."

"It does not look as if it is going to rain," Gerard said. "It was terribly hot riding here and both Rolla and I were pretty well done in by the time we reached Windsor."

"You rode Rolla the whole way? Oh, Gerard, how could you?"

"I rested him while I had something to eat and rode him carefully for the last five miles," her brother answered. "I also came across country, which is shorter, as you well know. I cannot afford to have more than one horse in London at the same time."

"Yes, I know that, but it is really too far for him."

"And for me!" Gerard replied. "I suppose there is no chance of a bath?"

"Of course there is, if you do not mind a cold one."

"I should welcome it."

"I will go and get it ready for you," Demelza said, "but you will have to get a bottle of wine for yourself. There is very little in the cellar, but I suppose His Lordship will be bringing his own."

Gerard grinned.

"He will be very thirsty if he survives on what we can provide."

Demelza reached the door.

"You have not told me how many there will be in the party."

"Six with me!"

"And will you be here for dinner?"

Gerard shook his head.

"I am going over to see Dysart at Winkfield to tell him that the Earl will be staying here. He is dining with him on Tuesday after the Grafton Sweep, which the Duke of York is quite convinced he will win because he has drawn Trance."

"I expect he will with Trance," Demelza said reflectively. "Is there a lot of money on him?"

"Thousands!" her brother answered.

The way he spoke made Demelza glance at him sharply.

"How much have you risked?"

"There is no risk where Trance or Moses is concerned, as you well know," he answered.

Demelza, though she wished to argue with him, knew that he spoke the truth.

Trance was an exceptional horse, and the Duke of York had won the Derby with Moses the previous year.

With the exception of Crusader, the latter was the most outstanding animal amongst all the highly bred ones which would be seen at the race-meeting.

As Demelza hurried upstairs to open up the bedrooms, many of which had not been in use for a long time, she was thinking with interest and excitement about the horses she would see in two days' time.

To her they were far more important than the crowds of distinguished people who watched them race, and to think that Crusader would actually be stabled at the Manor was a thrill beyond anything she had known for a long time.

She longed to talk about it with Abbot, but she knew that first she must prepare the house for the Earl and his guests and she only hoped he would not feel that his money had been mispent.

To her the large but low rooms, with ancient carved panelling on the walls and huge four-poster beds whose canopies touched the ceiling, were an enchantment that she loved and which had always been part of her life and her imagination.

Now as she drew back the curtains, many of which were worn, and threw open the diamond-paned windows, she wondered if the Earl, who was so rich, would only see how shabby everything was.

Perhaps he would not notice the mellow beauty of the faded tapestries, the colour of the polished floors, or the soft shades of many of the rugs which lay on them.

To Demelza there was beauty everywhere, just as there was the history of the Langstons in every room, in every picture, and in every piece of furniture.

One blessing, she thought, was that because it had already been such hot weather she had made fresh pot-pourri and most of the rooms were fragrant with it.

Her mother had taught her the secret recipe which had been handed down from their Elizabethan ancestors, just as there was a special one for the bees'-wax which polished the floor and the furniture.

There were also recipes for cordials, which she gave the villagers when they had an ailment which the doctor from Windsor thought beneath his condescension.

Everything was usually so quiet at the Manor. It stood on the very edge of Windsor forest, surrounded by trees, and although it was only a little over a mile from the race-course, the noise of the crowds did not encroach upon it.

But now, Demelza thought, it was somehow very exciting that the Manor should be drawn into the thrill of race-week.

She knew it was not only the thought of the house being ill-used which made her fight to stay when Gerard would have sent her away, but also that she could not have borne to miss the races.

She had attended them ever since she was a small child, and she loved every moment of it.

Now she knew that all along the edge of the course the tents and booths were going up, just as they did every year.

There would be every kind of refreshment for hungry and thirsty people; entertainers of all sorts—jugglers, glee-singers, and freaks; and a profusion of gaming tents, which as Demelza knew only too well fleeced all those who were foolish enough to risk their hard-earned savings.

Even Jem had been taken in last year by the thimble-game men, who were always numerous on the Heath. He had lost over a guinea trying to identify the thimble in the game which his grandfather had scornfully denounced as "a mug's game!"

Also arriving in their hordes would be the pickpockets and the thieves.

She and Nattie, who always accompanied her, were still laughing about the gang who, on a hot day such as they were likely to have this week, had made off with seventy great-coats stolen from carriages and stands.

But whatever happened it was all entrancing to Demelza and something to talk about and laugh over during the year which ensued until the next meeting.

"I could not bear to miss it," she said to herself, "and this year I shall not only see Crusader run, but I shall be able to talk to him and touch him when he is here in the stables."

What could be more fortunate, she thought, than that her grandfather, the spend-thrift who had wasted a great deal of money on slow horses and fast women, had also built for the former some very fine stables?

'Perhaps they will all be in use at the same time,' Demelza thought.

Her eyes were shining as she ran to the linen-cupboard to see if there was enough linen for the six beds which would be in use.

The sheets and pillow-cases all had lavender bags packed between them, which she had made the previous year.

She hesitated for a moment as she looked at one pile, separate from the others, which were edged with real lace. These had been her mother's pride and joy.

Then, almost beneath her breath, Demelza said:

"He is paying enough, he deserves them!"

She carried them into the Master bed-room, where the Langstons who owned the Manor had slept since Sir Gerard Langston had been given the Monastery and its grounds by King Henry VIII.

It was where Demelza's father had slept, but when Gerard had inherited he had preferred to keep his own room.

This was filled with all the things he had treasured ever since he was a small boy and the trophies he had won when he was at Oxford and racing his own horses in amateur steeplechases and point-to-points.

The Master bed-room was furnished with dark oak and the huge four-poster had the Langston coat-of-arms emblazoned on red velvet.

The curtains were drawn back and the windows were actually open when Demelza entered the room. She laid the sheets she carried down on the bed.

Because she had loved her father she had kept his things as he had always liked them; his ivory-backed brushes were on top of a high dressing-table and his polished riding-boots still stood in the wardrobe.

'I must move those,' Demelza thought to herself.

She picked them up and was about to carry them to one of the cupboards in the passage when she had a better idea.

She went towards the fireplace. On the right-hand side of it where the panel was exquisitely carved with flowers she put out her hand and pressed one of the petals.

Silently a whole section of the panelling opened. Inside was a flight of steps.

This was one of the secret staircases which Demelza had spoken of to her brother which led up to the very top of the house, where there was the Priests'-Room.

Used as a Chapel during the reign of Elizabeth, it had also secreted many Priests when the Catholics were persecuted and burnt at the stake, just as the Protestants had been under her sister Mary.

Langston Manor had in fact been one of the most notable secret hiding-places for the Jesuit Priests in the whole of England.

Demelza thought that some of the secret staircases had been built before that time, perhaps by the Monks who wished to keep watch on the novices or perhaps for more-sinister reasons.

But during the reign of Queen Elizabeth the house had become a labyrinth of stairs and narrow passages with doors which opened into almost every main room in the house.

Gerard had been aware, as she was, that once she was sleeping in the Priests'-Room and using the secret staircases, it would be quite impossible for any outsider to have the slightest idea that she was in the house.

'Even if they do see me,' Demelza thought to herself with a smile, 'they will think I am the ghost of the White Lady.'

She told herself that she must remember to tell Gerard to refer laughingly to the Langston ghost, which was locally a famous legend.

The Langstons at the time of Cromwell had openly declared themselves uninterested in the policial fortunes of the country. Cromwellian troops had even, from time to time, been billeted in the house and on the grounds.

But the daughter of the Baronet had fallen in love

with a fugitive Royalist and had hidden him in the Priests'-Room.

Unfortunately, one day when she was away from home, he was betrayed by a treacherous servant.

Dragged out by the troops, he had been executed on the spot, his body buried before she returned.

Legend related that, distraught by not knowing what had occurred, the lady had finally died of a broken heart, but her ghost continued to seek her lover.

Demelza had never actually seen the White Lady herself, although she had sometimes imagined that she felt her in the Picture Gallery late at night and heard her footsteps moving behind her on the twisted staircases which led to the Priests'-Room.

But the maids, especially the younger ones, continually shrieked out that they had seen the ghost, and even Nattie had at times admitted to a cold feeling between her shoulder blades and complained that she felt as if a ghost was walking over her future grave.

"I shall feel like a ghost," Demelza told herself, "when they are having a party in the Dining-Room and I am shut outside and cannot take part in it."

Then she laughed, because it did not trouble her in the least that she could not be invited to the parties that the Earl would be giving, while she could be with Crusader and his other horses in the stables.

'Abbot will be able to tell me all about them,' she thought, knowing that in most cases if they had run in any major race she would already know how they were bred and who had sired them.

"Could anything be more thrilling?" she asked aloud.

She looked at the velvet cover on the big bed, which had once been red but had now faded to a lovely shade of pink, thinking that the owner of Crusader would sleep there.

'Tomorrow,' she decided, 'I will pick some of the

roses which are exactly the same colour and put them on the dressing-table.'

She wondered if the Earl would notice.

Then she told herself it was very unlikely he would notice anything except that the ceiling was stained with damp and one of the gilt handles was lost off the chest-of-drawers.

"Why should we apologise?" Demelza asked herself disdainfully. "He will certainly be more comfortable than he would have been at the Crown and Feathers, and even if he does not like it, there is nowhere else he can go."

Some pride within herself made her almost resent the fact that they had to take money from a man who was so rich while they were so poor.

"Our family is as good if not better than his," she said aloud, and lifted her little chin higher.

Then she heard Gerard calling her, his voice echoing up from the hall.

She ran down the corridor to lean over the bannister.

"What is it?" she asked.

"I want to talk to you," he replied. "And what about my bath?"

Demelza started guiltily.

She had forgotten, in her aniexty to open the rooms, that Gerard wished to bathe.

"It will be ready for you in a few minutes," she promised.

She rushed to his room to pull from the cupboard the big circular tin bath in which he bathed when he was at home.

She set it down on the hearth-rug, laid a bath-mat and white towel beside it, and, still running as quickly as she could, went down the back stairs.

Fortunately, at this time of the day old Jacobs

thought that most of his chores were done, and so he was sitting, as she expected, in the kitchen, drinking a glass of ale and talking to Nattie.

Demelza burst into the huge kitchen with its flagged floors, and its long beams from which in prosperous days had hung hams, sides of bacon, and strings of onions, but which were now lamentably unencumbered.

As she entered, Nattie looked up at her in surprise.

She was only fifty years of age but her hair was streaked with grey. With her clean apron and rather severe face she looked exactly what she had always been, a child's Nurse, loving and tender, but at the same time strict as to discipline.

"What is it, Miss Demelza?" she asked in a surprised tone. "And your hair needs tidying!"

"Sir Gerard has come home, Nattie," Demelza said, and saw the older woman's eyes light up.

If there was one person in the world whom Nattie loved more than Demelza, who had been her baby from the time she was born, it was Gerard.

"Home!" she exclaimed. "I suppose he's on his way to stay with some of his smart friends."

"The Crown and Feathers burnt down last night," Demelza related breathlessly, "which means that all sorts of thrilling things are going to happen here."

"Here?" Nattie questioned.

"Sir Gerard wants a bath, Jacobs," Demelza said.

She knew that the old man, being rather deaf, had not heard her.

"A bath, Jacobs!" she repeated. "Will you take two cans of water upstairs to Sir Gerard's bed-room?"

Jacobs put down his glass.

He was an amenable old man, and reliable as long as he knew exactly what he had to do.

"Two cans, did you say Miss Demelza?"

"Two cans," Demelza repeated firmly.

He shuffled out of the kitchen, and Demelza, her eyes shining, began to tell Nattie of the excitements which lay ahead.

Chapter Two

"Will you drive me to Windsor Castle tomorrow?"

"No!"

"Why not? I felt sure you would be staying there when I learnt you could not go to Bracknell as you had intended."

"I have made other plans."

"Whatever they are, they must be in the vicinity of Ascot, and surely you can take me to the Castle on your way?"

It was difficult to imagine how any man could refuse Lady Sydel Blackford when she pleaded with him.

Lying back on a *chaise-longue,* she looked exceedingly alluring, wearing nothing but a diaphanous gauze negligee which clung to her perfect body.

She had been told so often that she resembled in face and figure the exquisite Princess Pauline Borghese, sister of Napoleon Bonaparte, who had been sculpted by Canova, that she almost instinctively fell into the same pose as the statue of the Princess.

Her golden hair was caught up on top of her head and her blue eyes looked at the Earl from under long, dark eye-lashes which owed more to artifice than to nature.

Everything about her was in fact slightly artificial, but at the same time there was no doubting her beauty or her sexual allure.

The Earl, however, leaning back in an arm-chair and sipping his glass of brandy, seemed for the moment immune both to her beauty and to the pleading in her eyes.

"Why do you not stay at the Castle?" she asked poutingly. "The King has asked you often enough to be his guest, and you know full well that he likes having you with him."

"I prefer to be on my own," the Earl replied, "especially in race-week, when I want to think about my horses."

"And not about me?" Lady Sydel enquired.

He made no reply and she said almost angrily.

"Why must you always be so irritatingly elusive? I would believe it was a pretence if it were not habitual."

"If I do not please you, there is an obvious answer," the Earl remarked.

Lady Sydel made a helpless gesture with her hands, her long fingers seeming almost too frail for the enormous rings she wore.

"I love you, Valient!" she said. "I love you, as you well know, and I want to be with you!"

"My party, as you are equally well aware, is a bachelor one," the Earl replied.

"And where will it take place now that you cannot go to the Inn at Bracknell as you intended?"

"I have rented Langston's house. It is, I believe, quite near the race-course."

"Langston? Do you mean that handsome boy who I understand has not a penny to bless himself with?"

"I imagine that is a fairly accurate description," the Earl replied dryly.

Lady Sydel laughed.

"In which case you will doubtless find yourself in some crumbling old Manor, extremely uncomfortable, with the rain leaking through holes in the roof and onto your head."

"It would undoubtedly please you if that proves to be the case."

"You had much better come to Windsor Castle with me."

Her voice was very soft and alluring, but the Earl yawned and she said hastily:

"His Majesty is expecting you to dinner on Tuesday."

"I have told him that I will dine with him on Thursday, after I have won the Gold Cup."

"You are very sure of yourself!"

"I am sure of my horse, and that amounts to almost the same thing."

"It is so bad for you, Valient, that you should always win what you desire, whether it is a horse or a woman."

The Earl appeared to consider this for a moment. Then he replied cynically:

"I think the odds are on the latter category."

"I hate you!" Lady Sydel exclaimed. "And if you are thinking of Charis Plymworth, I swear I will scratch her eyes out!"

The Earl did not reply and after a moment Lady Sydel said:

"I think I know why you will not come to the Castle on Tuesday evening. You are dining with John Dysart, and Charis Plymworth is staying with him."

"If you know I am already engaged, why press me to accept another invitation?" the Earl enquired.

"I could hardly believe you would be so treacherous and so abominably cruel to me!"

The Earl raised his eye-brows and took a sip of his brandy before he said:

"My dear Sydel, I have never tied myself to any woman's apron-strings, and let me make it clear, once and for all, I am not tied to yours!"

"But I love you, Valient! We have meant so much to each other, and I believed that you loved me."

There was a break in her voice that was very moving, but the Earl merely rose to his feet and set his glass down on the mantelpiece.

"Dramatics, as you are well aware, bore me, Sydel. I will say good-bye and look forward to seeing you in the Royal Box at Ascot."

He bent to kiss her hand, but she held up her arms to him.

"Kiss me, Valient, kiss me! I cannot bear you to leave me. I want you! I want you desperately! I would kill you rather than let you love another woman!"

The Earl looked down at her, at the passion flaring in her eyes, at her head thrown back at the invitation in her arched, half-naked body.

"You are very beautiful, Sydel," he said in a voice which did not make the words sound particularly complimentary, "but at times your protestations of affection become a bore! I will see you at the races."

He walked without haste towards the door and without looking back left the room.

Alone, Lady Sydel gave a cry of sheer exasperation. Then with her clenched fists she pounded one of the silk cushions on the *chaise-longue* until, exhausted, she flung herself back to stare despairingly at the painted ceiling above her.

Why did the Earl always leave her frustrated and almost desperate?

She told herself that she had in fact been rather stupid with him. She should have known by this time, having had innumerable lovers, that when men are satiated by love-making they want to be soothed and flattered—not engaged in a controversy such as had just taken place.

But her insatiable jealousy made her indulge in scenes and sulks, which, while they had other men on their knees, invariably left the Earl unmoved.

"Curse him!" she exclaimed aloud. "Why should he be different?"

She knew the answer only too clearly: he was different!

Because of it, she had sworn that she would make him as slavishly enamoured of her as she was of him.

Yet it seemed that she had succeeded in making him her lover only when it suited him, and she was not sure that he was any more enamoured of her than he had been of dozens of other women.

Lady Sydel had originally been confident that where she was concerned everything would be different.

Was she not the most acclaimed beauty in the whole of the *Beau Monde?* Had not her looks and her fascination been extolled by every womanizer and roué? Was it not a fact that she had only to snap her fingers to have any man she fancied prostrate at her feet?

Yet she knew indisputably that the Earl eluded her.

Even when he made love to her, she realised, his mind, and certainly his heart, if he had one, was not hers. She now thought despairingly that since Lady Plymworth had appeared on the scene he was not even as attentive as he had been in the past.

"I hate her! God, how I hate her!" Lady Sydel cried.

She had only to think of Charis Plymworth with her dark red hair and slanting green eyes to feel murderous.

"I will kill her, and I will kill him!" she told herself, speaking with a ferocity that meant she was on the verge of one of her temperamental rages, which terrified her household and at times even herself.

Lying on the *chaise-longue*, she tried to imagine herself striking with a sharp knife the smile from Charis Plymworth's enigmatic face, then turning on the Earl.

She wondered what she would feel if she had him lying dead at her feet, the blood oozing from a wound in his heart.

Then she told herself that life without him would be insufferable, and somehow, by some means, she must ensure that he remained her lover.

"Charis Plymworth shall not have him!"

Her voice seemed to ring round the walls of her *Boudoir,* and to mingle with the exotic perfume she always used and the fragrance of the tuberoses with which, since someone had once told her they exuded the scent of passion, she always surrounded herself.

She rose from the *chaise-longue* to walk to a gilt-framed mirror which stood at the end of the room.

She stood in front of it, looking at the curves of her body, which men always described as belonging to a Greek Goddess, at the round white column of her neck, and at the passion which still lingered in her eyes and on her lips.

"He can rouse me as no other man has done before," she told herself. "I cannot lose him. I will not lose him!"

* * *

The Earl, driving himself in his high-perch Phaeton, wondered why women always became abandoned either mentally or physically after they had been unusually passionate during the act of love.

It seemed to release something within them which at other times they kept under control.

He decided that he was already bored with Sydel's clinging possessiveness and almost insane jealousy.

'I was a fool to have become involved with her,' he thought.

He decided that when he returned to London from Ascot he would not call again at her house in Bruton Street, where the gossips said spitefully that the steps were almost worn away with her lovers tramping in and out.

"She is beautiful," he told himself, "but that is not everything."

Knowing that the remark was banal, he smiled as he made it, then asked himself what he did want from a woman.

There had been so many in his life, but always after a very short while he grew bored, as he knew now he was bored with Sydel Blackford.

But Charis Plymworth was waiting for him. She had made that clear at their last meeting, and he would see her on Tuesday night when he dined with Lord Dysart.

It might be rather difficult to say anything very intimate on that occasion, for he had the idea that Dysart rather fancied Charis, and if he did, there was no reason why he should not marry her.

The Earl was aware that Charis, like Sydel, was looking for a husband.

They were both widows, but while Sydel Blackford's aged husband had died of a heart-attack, leaving her exceedingly wealthy, Lord Plymworth had been killed two years ago and Charis was not well off.

The Earl, with a little smile, dwelling on her red hair and green eyes, thought it would be amusing to dress her.

Long experience had made him an expert in

what became a woman, and he had paid too many dressmakers' bills for them not to respect his judgement and hastily put his suggestions into operation.

'Green,' he thought. 'And naturally she will desire emeralds to wear with it. Peacock-blue would also be exceedingly effective, and diamonds to glitter in her small ears and against her hair.'

He hoped that when she let it down it would be long, soft, and silky,

Sydel's hair was thick but not particularly soft beneath his hands.

He remembered one woman—what the devil was she called?—who had hair which was like pure silk and which reached below her waist.

"Cleo? Or was it Janice?" He never had been good at names.

With a start the Earl realised that while he had been deep in his thoughts, although he had been driving superbly at the same time, he had reached Trevarnon House in Grosvenor Square.

Large and impressive, he had improved it out of all recognition after he had inherited from his father, and, like the Prince of Wales, he had collected pictures that were the envy and the admiration of a great many connoisseurs.

He had, as it happened, a number of family postraits that were unique in themselves.

There was the first Earl of Trevarnon, painted by Van Dyke, those that followed him by Gainsborough, Reynolds, and a recent one of himself by Lawrence because the Regent had insisted upon it.

The Earl entered the large hall in which stood a number of statues that he had also bought with discrimination.

His Major-Domo hurried forward to take his high-crowned hat and gloves.

"Have you arranged everything for tomorrow, Hunt?" the Earl asked.

"Everything, M'Lord."

"As I told you, there are few servants at Langston Manor, so we shall have to make up any deficiencies."

"I've seen to that, M'Lord. The Chef is bringing two kitchen-boys with him, and the footmen I've chosen are not above giving a hand in the household if necessary."

"Thank you, Hunt. And, as you are coming yourself, there will be no need for me to give the arrangements another thought."

"No, M'Lord. And I've made sure the Chef will bring most of the food he requires for your party. In race-week it'll be difficult to purchase anything locally."

"I am sure it will be," the Earl replied.

As he spoke, he walked away towards his Library, dismissing the problem of Ascot from his mind as he dismissed the thought of Lady Sydel.

Hunt would see to everything. He always did.

Nevertheless, on the following morning the Earl decided that he would arrive early at Langston Manor, before his guests were expected.

Like all born organisers, he could not resist, even with the most experienced servants, Major-Domos, and Comptrollers, checking things for himself.

A perfectionist in many ways, he saw no reason to suffer any discomfort if it was unnecessary.

If during the five days he was to spend at Ascot there was anything lacking he had not thought of, he could send a groom back to London. His Comptroller would see that it was despatched to him immediately.

He prided himself that he had been rather clever in finding at the very last moment an alternative to the Crown and Feathers.

He was well aware that there was not a house in

the vicinity of Ascot, from Windsor Castle to those
belonging to or hired by his friends, in which he
would not be a welcome guest.

But he had long made it a rule that where large
race-meetings were concerned he preferred to be with
his horses and independent of other people's whims
and fancies.

He also found that women were a distraction he
could well do without when he wished to concentrate
on the racing.

Soon after breakfast, at which he ate sensibly and
well, drinking coffee and not alcohol, he set off from
London, tooling a team of chestnuts that were the
envy of every Corinthian in the whole of Saint
James's.

He would have liked to drive six horses as he was
accustomed to do in competition with the Prince
of Wales, who had been painted in a high-perch
Phaeton driving to Ascot, with, of course, an attractive woman beside him.

But the Earl had learnt of old that on the crowded
roads round Ascot six horses could be an encumbrance
and would restrict the pace at which he travelled
rather than add to it.

It was a sunny day and already exceedingly hot,
and the road as the Earl had anticipated, was crowded
with coaches, tilburies, chaises, carts, and gigs.

As he drew nearer to Ascot, having twice changed
horses on the way so as not to slow the pace at which
he wished to travel, he was amused to notice slow-
moving wagons covered with leafy branches of trees
to protect the loads of countryfolk from the heat of
the sun.

These vehicles were so overcrowded that the Earl's
lips tightened at the thought of the suffering that was
being caused to the wretched animals which drew
them.

There were a number of Phaetons similar to the Earl's and splendid barouches with painted panels displaying the crests or coats-of-arms of their owners.

There were naturally a number of horses at which the Earl gave a second glance, only to decide that they did not equal his own.

He drew nearer to the course and began to look for the turn which Gerard Langston had told him would lead him to the Manor.

The thick fir trees of Windsor Forest bordered the road on either side until so unexpectedly that he almost missed it, the Earl saw a dusty lane winding into the wood.

He supposed that this was where he was intended to go, and he slowed his team, hoping as he did so that he would not be obliged to turn round, as this appeared to be an impossibility amongst the tree-trunks.

Then in front of him he saw two ancient lodges which appeared to be uninhabited and some iron gates which fortunately were open.

"This must be Langston Manor," the Earl told himself.

He thought that the appearance of the lodges and gates did not auger well for the condition in which he might find the house itself.

If Sydel was right, it would prove to be a crumbling Manor, with holes in the roof and perhaps too small for his party.

For a moment as he drove down the moss-covered drive, the Earl regretted that he had not accepted the King's invitation to Windsor Castle. At least there he would have a comfortable bed.

Then with a twist of his lips he thought that if Sydel had anything to do with it he would not spend much time in it, and he decided that however uncomfortable he was he would rather be on his own.

The drive turned, and suddenly he saw in front of him Langston Manor.

It was not in the least what he had expected and was indeed far more attractive than he had imagined possible.

It stood surrounded by trees and he saw at a glance that it was not only very old but also larger than he had thought it would be.

Spread out in front of him, the sun glinting on its diamond-paned windows and the pigeons sitting on its gabled roof, it seemed to the Earl as if it were something that had stepped out of a fairy-story.

He almost expected it would vanish and he would find himself staring at the ruins of what had once stood there.

But he knew he was being imaginative and it was in fact real, although it seemed impossible that he had been coming to Ascot all these years and had never been aware of its existence.

He thought too that it was very quiet and peaceful as there appeared to be nobody about.

He remembered how at other places he had stayed there had invariably been the noise of carriages grooms, and ostlers hurrying and scurrying, their voices shouting as he appeared.

Driving slowly so that he could take in the house and its surroundings, the Earl finally drew his team to a standstill outside the front door.

His groom jumped down from the back of the Phaeton and as he went to the leader's head the Earl said:

"We must find someone, Jim, to direct us to the stables."

"Oi thinks they be over there, M'Lord," Jim replied.

He pointed as he spoke and the Earl could see now a roof a little beyond the house.

"I will ask," he said.

He walked in and found himself in a hall with a carved staircase curving up to the first floor.

It was very attractive and the Earl was instantly aware of the fragrance of flowers and saw that they came from a bowl of red and white roses arranged on a table at the bottom of the stairs.

It encouraged him to see that the house was as attractive inside as was its outer appearance. It struck him that it was a home, and he wondered if young Langston had a mother.

He walked across the hall and looked into what he saw was the Drawing-Room.

Again there were flowers arranged on tables, and through the open French windows he could see a garden which was a riot of colour with great banks of crimson rhododendrons interspersed with bushes of syringa and white lilac.

The Earl's eyes came back to the room.

He saw that it was shabby, but at the same time everything in it was in perfect taste.

The pictures on the panelled walls needed cleaning, but he had a feeling that they would be interesting to look at more closely later.

Retracing his steps he found himself in the Library and knew instantly that this was the room he would make exclusively his own.

He liked the comfortable leather arm-chairs and the big flat-topped desk which stood in exactly the right place for the light.

There was still nobody about, and, because he was curious about the rest of the house, he did not go towards the kitchen-quarters where he was certain he would find what servants there were.

Instead, he walked up the staircase, noting that each oak pillar had originally been surmounted by a carved figure, although some were missing or damaged.

At the same time he appreciated its age and the way the wood had mellowed.

There were also pictures on the stairs, and as they were mostly portraits he guessed they represented Langston's ancestors, and he thought he recognised a resemblance in some of them to Gerard's handsome features.

At the top of the staircase he had the choice of going right or left. He chose the left, and moving down the low-ceilinged, narrow corridor saw in front of him a long Gallery.

It was the type of Gallery which Elizabethans had always built in their houses and into which on the long cold winters they moved their four-poster beds clustering them round the great fireplace and pulling their curtains for privacy.

In one of the houses he owned the Earl had a Gallery rather like it and he would often visualise the householders encamped there, the most important being nearest the fire.

He reached the door of the Gallery and saw that the sun was glinting golden through the windows on the polished floor.

Then at the far end he saw a woman in a white gown and thought he had at last found someone to tell him what he wished to know.

He moved forward, but even as he did so he realised that she had vanished!

He thought for a moment that, not having heard his approach, she must have sat down on a chair or sofa. Then as he walked farther down the Gallery he saw that it was in fact empty.

"I must have been dreaming," he told himself.

As he stood near the place where she had seemed to be standing, he heard a voice behind him say.

"Good-afternoon, Sir."

He turned round and saw an elderly woman wearing a grey dress and over it a white apron.

As he looked at her she curtseyed and said:

"I think you, M'Lord, must be the Earl of Trevarnon, who has taken the Manor for race-week. Sir Gerard told me to expect Your Lordship, but you are earlier than we anticipated."

"I hope that will not inconvenience you," the Earl said, "but I came ahead of my party to see that everything was in order."

"I hope it'll be, M'Lord," Nattie replied, "but we're very short-handed, as doubtless Sir Gerard informed you."

"He did," the Earl answered. "But my Major-Domo is on his way with a large number of servants to do everything that will be required."

"Thank you, M'Lord. And would Your Lordship like to see the bed-rooms?"

"I would!" the Earl replied.

Nattie led him along the corridor, in the opposite direction from which he had come, to the Long Gallery.

He wondered if he should mention that he had seen a young woman in white, but instead he remarked:

"Perhaps you would tell me who actually is in the house besides yourself?"

"Only old Betsy, who'll help in the kitchen if necessary, M'Lord," Nattie replied. "Then there's Jacobs, who's an odd-job man and brings in the coals and wood and carries up the bath-water."

The Earl did not speak and Nattie went on:

"There's Abbot in the stables, and his grandson Jem, who'll be riding our horse at the races."

She spoke in a way which told the Earl she was determined not to be intimidated or overpowered by his horses.

There was a faint smile on his lips as he replied:

"And perhaps now you will tell me your name and your position in the household?"

"I was Nurse to Master Gerard, M'Lord, and ever since he was a baby he's called me 'Nattie' because he couldn't say 'Nurse,' and the name's stuck."

"Then Miss Nattie it must be," the Earl said.

"Thank you, M'Lord. This is the room in which we thought you'd be most comfortable. It's the Master's Room, but Sir Gerard still prefers to be where he slept as a boy."

The Earl, despite what Demelza had anticipated, appreciated the big four-poster with its faded velvet curtains and cover, the beautifully carved panelling and the vase of pink roses which stood on the dressing-table.

"The flowers all over the house are delightful, Miss Nattie," he said. "Do I thank you for the arrangement?"

There was just a moment's hesitation before Nattie replied:

"I do them when I've the time, M'Lord."

"Then let us hope you will find time while I am here," the Earl. said.

Nattie told him where he would find the stables and he went downstairs to discover that Abbot had already shown Jem where to put the team.

The Earl inspected the rest of the stables.

They were surprisingly spacious, far better than he had expected to find, except in one of the great houses in this particular vicinity.

While he was in the stables his horses arrived.

By the time he had watched them bedded down and found that Crusader was in splendid shape, his staff were at the Manor and the Major-Domo was directing operations like a General in command of an Army.

Because there was nothing to do until his guests arrived the Earl walked into the garden to stand looking at the rhododendrons, the flowering shrubs, and the laburnum trees, which as a child he had called "golden rain."

It seemed to him as he moved towards them that he stepped back into the past and was in a land peopled by gnomes and fairies, dragons and Knights.

As a small boy he had always imagined that fire-breathing dragons lurked in the forests and there were elves burrowing under the mountains or hiding in the trunks of great trees.

He had not thought of such things for years, but now this mysterious house with its overgrown garden seemed hardly to belong to the modern world in which he lived.

It certainly had nothing to do with the men and women of the *Beau Monde* who would be converging on Ascot to spend a week not only racing but at parties, Balls, and, as far as the menfolk were concerned, riotous drinking and gambling.

But here there was only the sound of the wood-pigeons in the trees and the rustle of small animals moving beneath the shrubs.

The fragrance of the flowers was very different from the exotic perfumes used by Sydel and Charis and all the other women he knew.

The Earl walked a long way into the wood before finally he turned back.

Then when he came again in sight of the house, the same feeling of mystery and magic he had felt when he first saw it from the other side swept over him.

Absurdly, for one moment he wished that he could be alone there.

Then he laughed at himself and walked on quickly,

feeling certain that by this time his friends would have arrived.

They were in fact waiting for him in the Drawing-Room, sprawling comfortably in chairs, glasses in their hands, which were being continuously replenished from the bottles of champagne that stood in the ice-coolers on one of the side-tables.

"We were told you were here!" Lord Chirn exclaimed as the Earl entered through one of the windows, "but nobody knew where you had gone."

"I have been inspecting the property," the Earl replied. "Nice to see you, Ramsgill, and you, Ralph! How are you, Wigdon?"

He spoke last to Sir Francis Wigdon, a man he had not known for long but found amusing and who was with the cards as expert as he was himself.

"You have certainly found a very attractive house," Sir Francis replied, "and, in my opinion, far preferable to the Crown and Feathers!"

"We all agree on that," the Honourable Ralph Mear cried. "It is so like you, Trevarnon, to find something so unique and comfortable, when anyone else who had been burnt out in the same circumstances would be having to put up a tent on the Heath."

"Thank God we are saved from that!" the Earl replied, before pouring himself a glass of champagne. "I imagine the crowds will be worse this year than ever!"

"They increase year by year," Lord Ramsgill said, "and my grooms tell me there has been the usual number of accidents on the way here."

Accidents on the road were commonplace and during Ascot week when drivers poured gallons of beer down their throats to sweep away the choking dust there were always deaths through careless driving or merely because the congestion made them inevitable.

Twice the Royal Carriages returning from Windsor after the racing had been involved in fatal accidents. The first was a postilion who was unseated and the wheel of the carriage ran over him and killed him.

In the second case, a Member of the Household in attendance on the King had knocked over and killed a pedestrian.

It was something that had to be expected, but unfortunately it did not make those who drove any more careful the following year.

"What tips have you got for us, apart, of course, from recommending your own horses?" Lord Chirn asked the Earl.

"I think really you should be asking the Duke of York," he replied. "He told me the night before last that he means to make a killing this Ascot, and I cannot think of anyone likely to stop him."

"That means," Lord Ramsgill said, "that you and he will be backing the colt Cardenio, which he has entered for his own Selling Plate, and Moses."

"Most certainly Moses!" the Earl said. "Nothing short of breaking the Tablets of the Ten Commandments over his head is likely to stop him from walking off with the Albany Stakes."

They all laughed and the Earl sat down with his glass in his hand.

*　*　*

Upstairs in the Priests'-Room, Demelza wondered how she could have been so stupid as to have been nearly caught unawares by the Earl.

The sound of his footsteps entering the Gallery had alerted her.

She had one quick glance at a man who was handsome, tall, broadshouldered, and extremely elegant, before with a swiftness born of fear she had

slipped back through the panel and shut the secret
door soundlessly behind her.

She had had no idea that he was expected so early
and she had in fact only just finished arranging the
flowers.

She had then gone to the Long Gallery to collect
the book she had left there when Gerard had called
her on the previous day.

She had already moved everything else she wanted
up the twisting narrow stairs. Fortunately, her own
bed-room was not required for any of the guests, so
there was no need to hide her special treasures away.

Gerard had come back last night and left again
early this morning with last-minute instructions that
no-one was to be aware of her very existence.

"Why should anyone suspect me of having a sister
when they have never seen her in London?" he asked.

To Nattie he said:

"You and Betsy look after me here, and when I
come home I am alone with you. Is that clear?"

"Quite clear, Master Gerard," Nattie replied, "and
I think you're absolutely right. I don't want Miss
Demelza mixed up with any of those raffish friends
of yours."

"How do you know they are raffish, Nattie?"
Gerard asked.

"I've heard enough of the goings-on in London to
know what I think!" Nattie replied.

Gerard laughed and called her a prude, but as he
said good-bye to Demelza he said:

"Now obey me or I will be very angry. I will not
have you meeting Trevarnon or anyone else who is
staying in the house!"

"It seems to me that if these friends of yours are
so wicked, you might find a few better ones!"
Demelza remarked.

"They are all jolly fine fellows and excellent sportsmen," Gerard said quickly.

She had known he would spring to the defence of his friends, and she replied:

"I am only teasing, dearest, but do not drink too much. You know it is bad for you, and Mama always hated men who were hard drinkers."

"Trevarnon is not a hard drinker," Gerard said reflectively. "He is far too keen a pugilist for that, besides being the Champion Fencer at the moment."

It was not surprising, Demelza felt as he rode away, that he left her curious about the Earl.

There was apparently nothing at which His Lordship did not excel, besides being the owner of the most magnificent horse in the whole of Great Britain.

"Is Crusader better than Moses?" she asked Abbot.

"They've not run against each other yet, Miss Demelza," Abbot replied, "but if they do I'd bet me money on Crusader."

"Who is he competing against in the God Cup?"

"Sir Huldibrand. That's 'is only real challenge," Abbot answered.

"The horse belongs to Mr. Ramsbottom," Demelza remarked. "I do hope he does not win!"

"He's a good horse," Abbot said, "and Buckle's riding 'im."

Frank Buckle was one of the greatest jockeys of the time, and Demelza, who had seen him ride at other Ascot meetings, knew that he rode at only eight-stone-seven without wasting.

He had in fact been one of her heroes for many years, and she had heard someone say: "There is nothing big about Frank Buckle except his heart and his nose!"

His integrity was famous as well as his last spurt at the finish of a race.

Gerard had told her there was a couplet written about him:

> A Buckle large was formerly the rage
> A Buckle small now fills the Sporting Page.

Demelza had laughed and remembered it.

Now he was getting older, and although she felt it was disloyal she did want Crusader, because he was staying in their own stables, to win the Gold Cup.

As she walked back to the house she admitted that she was not only thinking of Crusader but also of his owner.

Everything Gerard had told her about the Earl had, despite his warnings, intrigued her.

"I have to see him!" she exclaimed, and remembered it would be easy to do so secretly at any time she wished.

Now she recalled that she had nearly met him face to face and was aware how furious Gerard would have been with her!

'This is a warning,' she thought. 'I must never take such risks again and must always be on my guard.'

At the same time, drawn irresistibly towards the man she longed to see, she crept very quietly down the twisting staircase until the sound of laughter told her that, as she had expected, the gentlemen were all congregated in the Drawing-Room.

She had spent as long as she could tidying it, dusting, and arranging the flowers.

She stood for a moment in the darkness, listening to the different sounds of the gentlemen's voices and trying to guess which one belonged to the names which Gerard had given her.

Her brother was not yet back. That meant that there were five men in the Drawing-Room.

She put out her hand to find one of the tiny peep-

holes which the Monks or the Priests had made in the
panelling so that they could look into every room.

It had been placed at eye-level for a man, which
meant that Demelza had to stand on tip-toe in order
to look through it.

It was so small, and concealed in the ornamen-
tation in the centre of a flower, that it was quite impossible for anyone in the room to notice it. In fact
Demelza had often found it difficult to remember
where it was when she was in the Drawing-Room.

She put her eye to the minute hole and the first
face she lighted on was that of a man of about
thirty-five years of age.

He was not in the least good-looking, but had a
benign appearance and was laughing uproariously at
something which had been said.

She guessed, although she was not certain, that
this was Lord Chirn.

Next to him was sitting a man with small dark eyes,
a pointed nose, and a slightly exaggerated cravat.

As she looked at him someone remarked:

"I am sure you think so too, Francis." When he
replied, she knew he was Sir Francis Wigdon.

There was something about him she did not like,
but she was not certain what it was. She only thought
that while his lips smiled his eyes did not do so.

Then she looked a little towards the centre of the
group and knew at once that she was looking at the
Earl of Trevarnon.

He was exactly as she had imagined him before she
saw him in the Long Gallery. Exceedingly handsome,
with a broad, intelligent forehead, square chin, and
firm mouth, he had two deep lines of cynicism running from his nose to the corners of his lips.

It was a raffish face, cynical, and had a faint resemblance, Demelza thought, to the picture of Charles II
which hung on the wall by the stairs.

One of his friends said something which amused him, but he did not smile; he just twisted his lips, but at the same time there was a twinkle in his eyes.

"He is magnificent!" Demelza told herself. "And whatever Gerard may say . . . I like him!"

Chapter Three

As soon as Demelza knew that the gentlemen had gone in to dinner, she slipped down the secret passage to the ground floor and let herself out through a panelled wall into a passage which led to the garden door.

She had taken the precaution of putting a dark cloak over her gown just in case anyone should see her moving through the garden.

It would be unlikely, but, as all her gowns were white, she knew that she stood out against the dark green leaves of the shrubs.

Nattie, who made all her gowns, had found that the cheapest material to be found in the small shops at Ascot or in Windsor was white muslin.

She had fashioned them in very much the same shape for the last five years: falling from a high waist, they not only became Demelza but because she was very slender gave her an ethereal look which had an indescribable grace.

Shutting the garden door behind her but making sure that it was unlatched for her return, she moved through the bushes towards the stables.

She was quite certain that at this time of night the grooms, jockeys, and apprentices, having put the horses to bed, would all have hurried off to the Heath.

There, the booths would be bright with lights and doing a roaring business before the races started the following day.

She expected, however, that Abbot would stay in the stables, feeling sure that she would seize the first available opportunity of seeing the Earl's horses.

Abbot had been told that she was in hiding and he was on no account to mention to anyone her name or that the Manor was her home.

Abbot could be trusted in the same way that Betsy and Jacobs could, and Demelza was certain that where he was concerned there would be no gossip such as might be expected to take place in other houses.

She reached the stables, where all was very quiet. Then as she moved over the cobbled yard Abbot appeared, carrying a lantern in his hand.

"Oi thought ye'd not be long in coming, Miss Demelza," he said with the affectionate familiarity of an old servant.

"You knew I would want to see Crusader," Demelza answered.

"We be right proud t' have such a fine piece of horse-flesh 'ere," Abbot said.

There was a note in his voice which told Demelza, who knew him so well, that he was extremely impressed with the Earl's famous horses.

Abbot went ahead of her and led her inside the stable, where the stalls all opened onto a long passage running the whole length of it.

He opened the barred gate of the first stall he came to and Demelza saw the horse she had longed to see.

Jet black, with a star on his forehead and two white fetlocks, he was a magnificent animal!

She knew he was directly descended from Godolphin Arabia, the Arabian horse which had come to England in 1732 after many strange and unhappy adventures.

He had finally become the property of Lord Godolphin, son-in-law of Sarah, the famous Duchess of Marlborough.

Secretly, the Bedouin who was his constant companion allowed Godolphin Arabian to serve Roxana, a great mare, from whose foals had descended many of the celebrated Thoroughbreds on the Turf.

Demelza patted Crusader's arched neck, and as he nuzzled his nose at her she saw the muscles rippling under the polished shine of his dark coat.

"He is wonderful!" she said in an awe-struck voice.

"Oi'd an idea as ye'd think so, Miss Demelza," Abbot said, "an' Oi admits Oi've never seen a finer stallion in all me born days."

"He will win the Gold Cup ... I am sure of it!" Demelza exclaimed.

It was hard, after the magnificence of Crusader, to appreciate the merits of the Earl's other horses, but she knew that all of them were exceptional.

When finally they reached Firebird she felt ashamed that she could see so many faults in him.

She put her arms round his neck.

"We may admire our visitors, Firebird," she said in her soft voice, "but we love you! You belong to us and are part of the family."

"That's true," Abbot said, "and ye mark me words, Miss Demelza, Jem'll bring Firebird first past th' winning-post on Saturday."

"I am sure he will," Demelza replied, "and perhaps the Earl will see Jem win and offer him a ride on one of his horses."

"Ye can be sure that's what Jem's a-dreaming, Miss," Abbot said with a grin.

"Is there a horse of any importance in the race in which you have entered Firebird?" Demelza asked.

Abbot scratched his head.

"The Bard might be a danger, Miss, but 'e's a-getting on in years and Oi don't much fancy th' jockey as is a-riding 'im."

Demelza hugged Firebird again.

"I know you will win!" she whispered, and felt as if he responded to her confidence in him.

She had to go back again to Crusader's stall before she left the stable, but before that she looked at the Earl's magnificently matched team of bays with which he had arrived at the Manor.

"One does not often see four horses so identical," she said as she inspected them.

" 'Is Lordship's groom was a-telling me that th' chestnuts with which they started out from London be so exceptional that 'is Lordship's refused twice and three times their value."

"Who would not rather have horses than money?" Demelza laughed.

At the same time, she thought that Gerard could do with both, and she could understand how frustrating it was for him to be with friends who had so much while he had but one horse and had to count every penny.

She talked to Abbot for a long time about the next day's racing, then hurried back to the house in case any of His Lordship's grooms should return early from the Heath.

It was not as late as she had anticipated, and when she started to climb the secret staircase she passed a connecting one which led to the Dining-Room, and she heard laughter.

She knew then that she could not resist looking at the Earl again, and she let herself out onto the Minstrels' Gallery overlooking one end of the great

Dining-Hall which had once been the Refectory used by the Monks.

The Minstrels' Gallery had been added after the Restoration, when with the return of the "Merrie Monarch" Charles II everyone had wished to dance and enjoy themselves.

It had been elaborately carved by the great craftsmen of the day and it would have been impossible for someone seated at the dining-table below to know that anyone was hidden beyond it.

Looking through the screen, Demelza saw that because he was host at the party the Earl was at the top of the table in the chair that had always been occupied by her father.

High-backed and upholstered in velvet, it seemed a fitting background for the man who was now sitting there.

Never had she imagined that any gentleman could look so magnificent or so elegant in evening-clothes.

She had always admired her father when he had been dressed for some formal occasion, but the Earl would, she thought, be outstanding even at a Royal Party at Windsor Castle.

As she looked down at him he was laughing and for the moment it made him look younger and eased away the cynical lines that were otherwise so prominent on his face.

The servants had left the room and the gentlemen were talking over their port. Some of them were cracking walnuts, which filled two of the Crown Derby dishes which had been among her mother's most treasured possessions.

They were seldom used and Demelza thought she must remember to tell Nattie to remind the visiting servants to be especially careful of them.

The candelabra which had belonged to her grandfather had been brought from the safe and now lit the table, but the huge hot-house peaches certainly did not come from what remained of the broken greenhouses. Nor did the large bunches of muscat grapes.

Demelza was less concerned with what the gentlemen were eating than with the man who sat at the head of the table.

She found it difficult to take her eyes from him, and at first the conversation was just a burr of words to which she did not listen, until with a little start she heard the Earl ask:

"Have you any ghosts in this house, Gerard?"

"Dozens of them!" her brother replied. "But personally I have never seen one."

"What are they?" the Earl persisted.

"There is a Monk who is supposed to have hanged himself for the expiation of his sins," Gerard replied. "And there is a child who was burnt at the stake with his parents, by Queen Mary's Inquisition, and of course the White Lady."

"The White Lady?" the Earl asked sharply.

"She is undoubtedly, according to legend and local superstitions, our most famous ghost," Gerard said with a smile.

"Tell me about her."

Gerard told the story of the White Lady searching for her lost lover, and Demelza, seeing the Earl listening attentively, was sure he had in fact seen her in the Long Gallery, which would account for his interest.

She wondered if he would admit to having done so, but when Gerard finished the tale the Earl merely asked:

"To those who see the White Lady does it mean good fortune—or bad?"

"It means," Lord Ramsgill interrupted before Gerard could reply, "that they who see her will seek endlessly for love, which will always elude them."

He laughed.

"That is something which will never happen to you, Valient."

"It would do you good to be the hunter instead of the hunted for a change!" the Honourable Ralph Mear interposed.

"A hope that is as unlikely to be fulfilled as that Crusader will not win the Gold Cup," Lord Ramsgill remarked.

"I suppose you have all backed him?" the Earl asked.

"Of course we have," Lord Chirn said, "despite the fact that we got damned rotten odds! The trouble is, Valient, the book-markers are afraid of your unparalleled success and are not really anxious to take any bets on him."

Looking round the table, Demelza noticed that Sir Francis Wigdon had said very little.

He had the habit of sticking forward his lower lip which gave him a sinister, rather sardonic expression.

'I do not like him!' she thought again. 'There is something about him which is unpleasant.'

She thought him a contrast to the Earl's other guests, who seemed to be decent, sporting types such as her father's friends had been.

She was sure that Gerard would come to no harm with any of them except perhaps Sir Francis.

She did not know why she had taken such a dislike to him, but, perhaps because she spent so much time alone, she was very perceptive about people.

It was as if she could feel the auras that emanated from them and at times to be almost aware of what they were thinking.

"I am sure," she told herself now, "that while Sir Francis pretends to be his friend, he is jealous of the Earl. There is no warmth about him."

Then she told herself that it was time she went upstairs to bed, and she knew that as soon as the servants sat down to supper Nattie would bring her something to eat.

With one last look at the Earl, thinking again how authoritative and imposing he was, she slipped through the secret panel and found her way, with the surety of one moving in a familiar place, to the top of the house.

Nattie was there before Demelza arrived.

"Where have you been, Miss Demelza?" she asked in the severe tone that she always assumed when she was frightened.

"I have been to see the horses, Nattie, and Crusader is wonderful! The most magnificent horse you have ever seen!"

"You've no right to be walking about when you know what Master Gerard said to you."

"I was quite safe," Demelza answered. "There was only Abbot in the stables. Everyone else had gone to the Heath, and I knew the gentlemen were at dinner."

"When they are in the house you are to stay here in this room," Nattie said firmly.

"Stop worrying about me, dear Nattie," Demelza smiled, "and tell me what you have brought me to eat, for I am exceedingly hungry!"

"I thought you would be, and I managed to bring you a little of three of the many dishes they had for dinner."

Demelza lifted the silver lids which covered the dishes and gave a cry of delight.

"They look delicious! Do find out how to make them, Nattie, and we can try them out next time Gerard comes to stay."

"That's exactly what I thought," Nattie replied. "And now I'd better be going back."

"No, wait and talk to me for a moment," Demelza begged. "I am longing to hear everything that has happened. It will save you coming back a second time for the tray."

She knew by the way that Nattie set herself down on the rush-bottomed chair that she was only too willing to be encouraged to talk.

"I have to admit, Miss Demelza," she began, "that His Lordship's servants are helpful and exceedingly polite."

It was what might have been expected, Demelza thought.

As she ate, she listened attentively as Nattie told her about Mr. Hunt, the Major-Domo, the footmen who had told her they would help her with the beds, and the Chef, who had been with the Earl for many years and was undoubtedly a culinary genius.

"There's only one man I don't care for," Nattie chattered on, "and that's Mr. Hayes, the Under-Butler."

"The Under-Butler?" Demelza asked. "You mean to say there are two of them?"

"Apparently the old Butler, Mr. Dean, who was with His Lordship's father, suffers from the heat, and the Major-Domo brought his assistant with him. But there's something about him I don't care for, though I can't put my finger on it. He's polite enough."

Demelza thought with a smile that Nattie had the same instinct about the Under-Butler that she had about Sir Francis Widgon.

Doubtless, if anyone heard them saying such things, they would think she and Nattie were being spooky because they lived in such an old house.

'We will turn into a pair of witches, if we are not careful,' Demelza thought to herself, but aloud she said:

'.I expect he is efficient at his job and knows what wines suit His Lordship."

"Certainly enough bottles have arrived!" Nattie

exclaimed. "The cellar's almost full, and that's the truth!"

"Papa always said that racing was thirsty work," Demelza laughed, "and you and I will be thirsty tomorrow, if the dust is as bad as it usually is on the Heath."

"I was just thinking, Miss Demelza, it'd be a mistake for you to go to the races . . ." Nattie began.

"Not go to the races?" Demelza interrupted. "You must be crazy, Nattie! Of course we are going! We have always gone, and certainly nothing would stop me this year, when I want to see Crusader run . . . and of course Firebird."

"It's taking a risk," Nattie murmured.

"How could it be?" Demelza asked. "We shall be on the course and everyone who is staying in the house will be in the Royal Box with His Majesty."

That was so undeniably true that Nattie had nothing more to say.

"As soon as the gentlemen have left the house and the footmen have finished helping you make the beds," Demelza said, "we will slip down to the stables."

Her voice was excited as she went on:

"Abbot has promised to take us in the gig and he will park it well beyond the stands. In the crowds, I promise you, it would be a miracle if anyone paid any particular attention to us."

"I suppose you are right," Nattie admitted a little grudgingly. "I'll bring up a fresh gown in the morning, and you go to bed now straight away."

"I have every intention of doing so, " Demelza answered. "I want to dream about Crusader."

"Horses, horses! That's all you think of!" Nattie said. "It's time at your age you had something else to dream about."

Demelza did not answer.

She heard these words so often before from Nattie,

and she knew that her old Nurse deeply regretted the fact that they were unable to entertain what she thought of as "the right sort of people."

It was quite impossible, living alone at the Manor without a Chaperon, for her to meet girls of her own age or go to the Balls which occasionally took place in the countryside.

Most of the great houses, it was true, were full only during race-week, or when there was some important entertainment at Windsor Castle.

Even so, if Lady Langston had been alive there would have been parties in which Demelza could have taken part.

But their mother had died when Demelza was sixteen and still in the School-Room, and when Gerard had gone off to London it was impossible for Demelza alone to make any overtures to the people who lived round them.

In fact she did not even know who they were, since many of the houses had changed hands since her father had died.

Actually she had no desire to do anything other than live quietly at the Manor and ride Gerard's horses.

When he occasionally came home because he was unable to afford the expense of London, she was blissfully happy to ride with him over the Heath and in the forest and to listen eagerly while he told her stories of the gaiety of his life amongst the *Beau Mondo*.

Sometimes she wondered to herself what would happen if Gerard got married.

Then she knew that that was something he would certainly be unable to afford at the moment, in fact at any time, unless he married a rich wife.

She saw the expression on Nattie's face now, and as she kissed her good-night she said:

"Stop worrying, Nattie. I am happy. You know how happy I am."

"It's an unnatural way of living—that's all I can say, Miss Demelza!" Nattie said sharply.

Without waiting for an answer she went down the stairs to let herself out through the first secret door she came to, because, as she had often said: "Them secret passages give me the creeps!"

Alone, Demelza laughed fondly to herself because she loved Nattie, who gave her heart and soul to her "babies' interests."

Quickly her thoughts returned first to Crusader, then to his owner.

As she knelt to say her prayers she prayed that the great horse would win, but somehow as she conjured him up in her mind, the Earl stood beside him and the two seemed inseparable.

* * *

The next morning the Manor was full of bustle and excitement.

It was always the same the first day of race-week. Everyone was eager to be off and a dozen things seemed to have been overlooked at the last moment.

The Earl with his guests was lunching in the Jockey Club, while owing to the sunny weather the Heath would be covered with people of all classes having picnics.

The coaches which had been crowding in since first thing in the morning had huge hampers of venison, fish, and sweet-meats piled upon their roofs.

The tents and booths were stocked with food, and, because of the heat, casks of spruce-beer had begun to flow very early in the morning.

By the time Demelza and Nattie reached the course, the noise was deafening not only from the punters, the book-markers, and the "tic-tac men," but also from the entertainers.

Outside a Show Booth where a wide variety of freaks were to be seen, the public was being invited to enter for the expenditure of one penny.

They passed "the Bohemian," who balanced coach-wheels on his chin, and saw a number of women dancing on stilts eight feet high.

They not only made money by exercising their skill, but also, Demelza thought, they had the advantage of seeing the races over the heads of everyone else.

She was particularly interested to see the new Royal Box when it was filled with spectators, the most important of course being the King.

It had been started in May and had only just been finished last week in time for the races.

The King had employed as his architect the famous John Nash, who was responsible for the improvements to Buckingham Palace, the design of Regent Street, and what were called the "Nash Terraces" in Regent's Park.

Immediately opposite the winning-post, the Royal Box was built in imitation of a Greek portico with fluted pilasters supporting the roof.

It had two storeys, of which the upper part was used only by the King. During its construction Demelza had visited it and had seen that it had been divided into two rooms, which at the last moment had been fitted out with white muslin curtains.

Today it would have been impossible for her to get in, for round the Royal Stand there was a small enclosure guarded by Police Officers and gate-men and only those invited by the King were admitted.

On either side of the Royal Box were nine other stands of various sizes and they appeared already to be crammed to bursting. Demelza and Nattie looked at them with interest as they drove along the other side of the course.

"Oi thinks we'd be best off 'ere, Miss," Abbot said, drawing the gig to a standstill beyond a number of other carriages, coaches, and wagons.

"I thinks so too," Nattie said before Demelza could speak. "If we cross to the other side we'll not be able to get away quickly, and it's important we leave before the last race."

Demelza knew Nattie was worrying about getting home before the Earl and his party returned.

So she accepted that they should stay where they were, although she knew she might not be able to see the saddling, in which she had always been so interested in the past.

They were no sooner in place than there were cheers at the other end of the course, which they knew announced the arrival of the King.

Abbot had heard earlier in the week that His Majesty might not appear as he was suffering from a "severe and dangerous attack of gout."

However, he had undoubtedly arrived, but did not drive along the course as his father had always done. Instead he proceeded along the rear of the booths.

Demelza could hear the cheers all the way to the Royal Box, then the King appeared at the window and the gentlemen in the enclosure below all raised their hats to him.

He stood for some moments acknowledging the cheers, which were not very effusive, and Demelza could see that he was clad in the Windsor uniform with a single diamond star on his breast.

She wondered if the Earl was with him.

Nattie, who had always shown an intense interest in the Royal Party, recognised the Duke of York and the Duke of Wellington.

"Who is the lady beside the King?" Demelza asked.

"Lady Conyngham," Nattie replied in a repressed voice which told Demelza she did not approve of Her Ladyship.

As soon as the King arrived the first race was run, after which racing was interrupted by a one-hour interval for luncheon.

Nattie produced sandwiches, but Demelza looked rather longingly at the magnificent picnics which were laid out either in the carriages or on the grass.

There were cold brands of every sort, and bottles of hock and champagne were being opened on every side.

It was very hot, but the roar of cheers which went up as Trance, as was expected, won the Grafton Sweep was full-throated and uninhibited.

"That's three hundred guineas for His Royal Highness's pocket," Abbot remarked.

He had previously told Demelza that the Duke of York had backed Trance in the Sweep against a horse called The Duke.

Abbot had left Demelza and Nattie alone in the gig for some time before the race, and Demelza was quite certain that he also had backed Trance.

After one of the Earl's horses had won the third race of the day, Nattie insisted on their leaving, although Demelza longed to stay for the fourth and last race.

She tried to protest, but Nattie said firmly:

"Five days of racing's enough for anyone, and we're taking no risks. Come along, Miss Demelza, there's work for me to do at home, as you well know."

Because no-one else was leaving so early and the roads were clear, they got back to the Manor far more quickly than might have been expected.

"Thank you, Abbot," Demelza said as they drove into the yard. "It was very exciting and I loved every moment of it!"

"We'll see some fine racing tomorrow and Thursday," Abbott answered, "an' if Moses don't win the Albany Stakes—Oi'll eat me hat!"

"I am sure he will," Demelza said with a smile.

Then she was hurried by Nattie round the side of the house to the garden door.

In the passage she opened the secret panel while Nattie went off towards the kitchen-quarters.

It had all been very exciting, Demelza thought, as she began to climb the narrow staircase, but she was hot from the burning sun and stopped for a moment to take off her bonnet.

As she did so, to her surprise she heard a woman's voice say:

"As His Lordship is not at home, I would like to leave a note for him."

"Of course, M'Lady. There's a writing-desk in here," a servant answered.

Astonished that anyone should expect to find the Earl at home at such an hour in the afternoon before the racing was finished, Demelza moved a few steps until by using the peep-hole she could see into the Drawing-Room.

Moving into the room from the hall she saw the most beautiful woman she had ever seen in her life.

Wearing a gown of periwinkle blue which matched the colour of her eyes, her golden hair framed by a high-crowned bonnet covered in blue ostrich feathers, she was breathtaking.

There were diamonds round her neck and over the short gloves that covered her wrists.

She moved with a sinuous grace that struck Demelza as having something almost feline about it.

She reached the centre of the room, where Demelza could see her clearly. Then as the servant following her shut the door, she turned round to say in a different tone:

"Have you anything to report to me, Hayes?"

Demelza remembered that Hayes was the Under-Butler of whom Nattie had spoken.

"No, M'Lady, we only arrived yesterday and there're only gentlemen here. No ladies of any sort."

"Not living in the house?"

"No, M'Lady, only an old Nurse and another servant."

"Lady Plymworth has not called?"

"No, M'Lady."

The elegant visitor stood for a moment, her gloved finger against her chin, as if she was thinking, then she said:

"His Lordship is dining out this evening?"

"So I believe, M'Lady."

"Is it with Lord Dysart?"

"I heard His Lordship's valet mention that name, M'Lady."

"That is what I thought," the visitor murmured almost beneath her breath.

Then to the Under-Butler she said in a commanding tone:

"Now listen to me carefully, Hayes. His Lordship always has a glass of wine when he is dressing for dinner. I wish you to decant a bottle yourself and put into it before you take it upstairs the contents of this."

As she spoke, she drew from her reticule a small bottle about three inches high and held it out to the Under-Butler.

He hesitated.

"I wouldn't wish, M'Lady, to do anything . . ."

"It will not hurt him badly, you fool!" the lady said firmly. "His Lordship will just be unable to attend the party this evening and doubtless will have a head-ache in the morning."

She looked at the expression on Hayes's face and laughed.

"Do not worry yourself. You will not swing on Tyburn, that I promise you!"

"I'm—afraid, M'Lady! Suppose the wine was drunk by the wrong person?"

"If it is, you will suffer for it!" the lady snapped. "I got you this position and I have paid you well. You can expect further recompense if what you do is successful."

"Thank you, M'Lady. It's only that I like the post and don't want to leave it."

"You will leave it when it suits me!" the lady retorted. "Now, you understand exactly what you have to do?"

"Yes, M'Lady."

"So carry out your orders."

"I'll do my best, M'Lady."

"You had better do so!"

The visitor walked towards the door and as Hayes opened it she said:

"On second thought, as I may see His Lordship tonight I will not leave a note for him. What I have to tell him will be a surprise, so please do not inform him that I was here."

Demelza realised that these words were intended for the ears of the footmen on duty in the hall.

The lady went from the Drawing-Room and Hayes followed her, leaving the door open behind him.

Demelza waited.

After a little while she heard the sound of wheels and knew that a carriage was driving away from the front door.

She drew in her breath with a gasp, realising that she had held her breath for most of the time she had been listening.

How was it possible? How could such an exceedingly beautiful person as the lady intended to harm the Earl?

And in order to do so, she was intriguing with one of his own servants against him!

Dazed and bewildered, Demelza climbed up the stairs to the Priests'-Room and sat down on the bed to think.

It was nothing new, she remembered, for women to use drugs or medicines of some sort to hurt someone they either disliked or . . . loved.

It struck Demelza that that was the explanation why the beautiful lady who had come to the Manor wished to prevent the Earl from dining this evening with Lord Dysart—she loved him.

That was why she was jealous of Lady Plymworth of whom she had spoken.

But to drug the Earl! That was surely carrying jealousy to extremes!

Demelza could remember hearing her father discussing—years ago—the behaviour of Lady Jersey when Princess Caroline of Brunswick married the Prince of Wales.

Lady Jersey, who had apparently been in love with the Prince, had been one of the people he sent to meet his bride when she arrived in England.

Everybody knew later that Lady Jersey had put a strong emetic in the Princess's food to spoil the first night of the honeymoon.

Although Demelza had not yet been born at the time this had happened, she always felt it was what Gerard would call a "dirty trick." In fact she herself had felt that it was despicable and beneath the dignity of any woman who called herself a lady to sink to such tactics.

And yet here was someone, so beautiful that Demelza felt any man who saw her must be infatuated with such a lovely face, behaving in very much the same way towards the Earl.

Demelza felt she could not bear to think of the

Earl's suffering or of him lying unconscious on his bed.

He was so strong, so athletic, and as Gerard had said, "a Corinthian of Corinthians," that it would be like seeing the fall of a great oak tree to see him prostrate through the treacherous hand of a woman.

What was more she had said that it might give him a head-ache tomorrow.

Suppose he was too ill to see Moses run? Or, more important, his own horse who was entered for another race?

"It must not happen," Demelza said to herself positively. "I must stop it! I must!"

Her first thought was that she must tell Gerard, but this would present a number of difficulties.

First was that Gerard's bed-room was one of the few rooms in the house where there was not a secret entrance.

This was because one of the previous owners of the Manor had removed the oak panelling and had instead papered the walls with a very attractive rice-paper which he had brought back from China.

It was certainly very effective; at the same time, it prevented Demelza from being able to reach her brother unless she entered his room from the passage, which would be unthinkable.

Apart from that, she had a feeling that Gerard would not wish to be involved in such an explosive situation which centered round a beautiful lady who loved the Earl and had bribed one of his chief servants.

'No, I cannot tell Gerard,' Demelza decided.

But what else could she do?

She sat thinking for a long time, and finally made a decision.

* * *

The Earl came back from the races in extremely good humor.

He had enjoyed an excellent luncheon with the other members of the Jockey Club and had been entrusted by the King with the placing of his bets.

This had resulted in his handing over to His Majesty a quite considerable sum at the end of the day, while the Earl himself had backed three winners out of the four, which was certainly a good percentage.

He was also looking forward to the dinner-party tonight, when he would see Charis Plymworth again.

They had met in the Royal Box and she had intimated very clearly that she was as anxious to be with him as he was with her.

She was looking extremely beautiful, and the slant of her green eyes intrigued him as did the Sphinx-like smile which curved her red lips.

He had known as they talked together that he was being watched by Sydel, but it was difficult for her to make a scene in the King's presence, as the Earl was quite certain she wanted to do.

"Jealous women are a damned bore!" he said to Lord Chirn as they drove away from the race-course.

"All women are jealous," his friend answered, "but some more so than others!"

The Earl did not reply and Lord Chirn went on:

"Beware of Sydel Blackford! It is rumoured that she practises Black Magic and murmurs incantations over a dead cockerel—or whatever it is they do!"

The Earl laughed.

"That might have been possible in the Middle Ages, but I cannot believe any woman would go as far as that these days."

Lord Chirn smiled. He did not bother to tell the Earl that he himself had had a short but fiery affair with Lady Sydel and knew she was capable of anything and everything to gain her own ends.

He thought, as so many of the Earl's friends had thought before, that it was a pity he could not settle down and have a family.

Most men wanted an heir, and the Earl had so many possessions that it seemed a crime against nature that he should not have a son to inherit them.

Whatever Lord Chirn thought, however, he was not prepared to voice such sentiments aloud, and when they reached the Manor House they were talking about the racing.

There was champagne and sandwiches waiting in the Drawing-Room, but the Earl had already drunk enough in the Royal Box. After talking to his friends for a short time he went upstairs to dress.

He knew that his valet, Dawson, would have a bath ready for him. He was looking forward to cooling off after the heat of the day and getting rid of the dust, which, as he had anticipated, had been worse than usual owing to the long spell of dry weather.

His valet helped him out of his tight-fitting and well-cut coat which had been the envy of the King.

"I cannot think why Weston cuts so well for you and so badly for me!" he had grumbled.

The real answer, the Earl knew, was that the King had grown so extraordinarily fat in the last few years that it was impossible for any tailor to give him the elegant figure he craved. But aloud he said:

"I thought how admirably your uniform became you today, Sire."

His Majesty had smiled and preened himself.

"A good day's racing, Dawson," the Earl remarked now as he untied his cravat.

"Excellent, M'Lord!"

The Earl threw his discarded cravat down on the dressing-table and as he did so he saw a very small note propped against his gold-backed hair-brushes.

It was addressed to him and marked *Urgent!* in a hand-writing he had never seen before.

"Who left this, Dawson?" he enquired.

The valet turned to look at what he held in his hand.

"I've no idea, M'Lord. I've not seen it before."

"It was here—on my dressing-table!"

"No-one's brought it in while I've been 'ere, M'Lord."

The Earl opened the note.

There were only a few lines written in the same elegant but unfamiliar writing:

"Do not drink the wine you will be offered while dressing for dinner. It will make you ill."

The Earl stared at what he had read and as he did so there was a knock on the door.

Dawson went to it.

He came back carrying a salver on which was a cut-glass decanter and a single glass.

"Will you have some wine before or after your bath, M'Lord?" he enquired.

The Earl looked at the wine.

"I wish to speak to Hunt," he said. "Before he comes upstairs, ask him to find out who called here today and who left a note for me."

Dawson looked surprised, but, setting down the silver salver, he obediently left the room.

The Earl picked up the decanter and sniffed the wine. There appeared to be nothing unusual about it. Perhaps, he thought, the note was a joke, a trick played on him by one of his friends.

But he was sure the hand-writing did not resemble that of anyone staying in the house.

He was almost certain it had been inscribed by a woman.

Even as he thought that, he was conscious of a
subtle fragrance he had noticed before.

He held the note to his nose and found that it smelt
very faintly of some flower to which he could not put
a name.

Now it struck him that he had been aware of the
same perfume in his bed-room and in other parts of
the house.

He had thought that it came from the bowls and
vases of flowers that were arranged in every room,
but there were only pink roses here in his bed-room
and the fragrance on the note was not that of a rose.

It was all rather intriguing and he felt in some way
that it was a part of the mystery that was exemplified
by the house itself.

There was a knock on the door and the Major-
Domo stood there.

"You sent for me, M'Lord?"

"I wish to know who called here today, and who left
a note for me."

"I've learnt, M'Lord that Lady Sydel Blackford
called late this afternoon, but at her request this was
not reported to me until I made enquiries a few seconds ago."

Lady Sydel Blackford!

"And she left a note for me?"

"No, M'Lord. She expressly said that she wouldn't
leave a note because she'd a surprise for Your Lordship this evening and didn't wish to spoil it."

"It seems to me extraordinary that her visit was not
reported to you, Hunt."

"It was sheer incompetence, M'Lord, and I've already spoken to Hayes."

"The Under-Butler?"

"Yes, M'Lord. Apparently 'twas Hayes who let Her
Ladyship in."

"And who decanted the wine that was brought to my room this evening?"

The Major Domo looked surprised, but he answered:

"I'm afraid I've no idea, M'Lord, but I'll find out."

"Do that," the Earl said sharply.

Aain there was a wait. The Earl had undressed and had his bath, revelling in the cold water and getting Dawson to pour over him the last can before he stepped out to wrap himself in a towel.

He was still drying himself when the Major-Domo returned.

"I apologise, M'Lord, for taking so long," he said, "but it was with some difficulty that I discovered that the bottle of wine in question was decanted by Hayes and also was brought upstairs by him. He then handed the salver to Robert, who's on duty on this floor and who brought it to Your Lordship's room and handed it in."

"What do you know about Hayes?" the Earl asked.

"He came with excellent references, M'Lord, after Your Lordship thought with so much entertaining in the Season it was too much for Dean."

"What references did you take up on him?"

"Two, M'Lord. One from the Duke of Newcastle, which was excellent, and the second from Lady Sydel Blackford."

The expression on the Earl's face was that of a stalker who gets the stag he has been following within range of his rifle.

"Lady Sydel Blackford!" he exclaimed. "And it was she who spoke to Hayes this afternoon! Send the man up to me in five minutes!"

It was not difficult for the Earl to extort from Hayes all the information he required.

He then sent for the Major-Domo and told him to

dismiss the Under-Butler immediately, without a reference.

Looking as magnificent in his evening-clothes as Demelza had thought him to be last night, the Earl drove off towards Lord Dysart's house with a feeling of triumph.

He had found the culprit and he would take care in the future that no-one recommended by Sydel Blackford should cross the threshold of any house he possessed.

But one thing remained unsolved.

Who had written the warning note? Who had put it on his dressing-table? And who used the tantalising perfume to which he still could not put a name?

He found himself puzzling over the answer to these three questions the whole evening.

Somehow in consequence he found the enigmatic expression in Charis Plymworth's slanting eyes less mysterious and intriguing than he had expected.

Chapter Four

Returning from the races on Wednesday, Demelza felt it was one of the most exciting days she had ever spent.

She had not only seen the most superb horses, but she had also been thrilled in a manner that she had never known before by the knowledge that she had saved the Earl.

She could see him in the small enclosure outside the Royal Box and occasionally caught a glimpse of him in the window beside the King.

She watched him in the saddling enclosure after she had persuaded Nattie, much against her will, to cross the course with her.

"What'll Master Gerard say?" Nattie questioned.

"If he notices us, which is very unlikely, he will understand that I cannot bear not to see the horses at close quarters."

She particularly wanted to see a horse called Cardenio race against Mr. Green's horse, Trance.

She also knew that the breeding of both the horses was favoured against the cold entered by the Duke of York for his own fifty-pound plate.

It was run over two and a half miles, and the colt His Royal Highness had, which won, was a three-year-old bay by Election out of a Sorcerer mare.

Boyce, an apprentice whom Abbot had picked out as likely to be a well-known jockey in the future, rode extremely well.

When that excitement was over there was the Albany Stakes to watch, where again the Duke of York was victorious with his Derby winner, Moses.

Moses had been bred by him and was a bay. But although it was a superb animal and Demelza had been looking forward to seeing him, she decided he did not really measure up to Crusader.

She was sure the Earl was winning his bets, and when she saw him talking to Gerard she hoped that her brother was taking advantage of his superior knowledge of the Turf before he expended their precious money with the bookies.

Nattie took her to the far end of the saddling enclosure, as far away as possible from the social viewers who were crowded at the other end nearest to the stands.

The gentlemen who attended the King looked exceedingly smart and wore their high-crowned hats at a rakish angle that was fashionable.

But Demelza felt that not one of them could equal not only the elegance of the Earl but his air of consequence, which seemed an inescapable part of him.

Again Nattie insisted they should leave immediately after the third race, and although Demelza longed to plead for them to stay a little longer, she knew in fact that it was prudent not to take any risks.

She had not spoken to Gerard since the Earl and his party had arrived at the Manor and she knew that her brother was deliberately pretending to himself that she was not in the house.

She could not help wondering why he was making

such a fuss, for the Earl's guests behaved in the most decorous manner.

There was no hard drinking, which Demelza had been told was traditional among the Bucks of St. James's.

What was more, there were no riotous parties, which, she had heard, invariably took place in most other houses in race-week.

Last night the Earl had been out to dinner, but to-night he was dining at home and Demelza wondered if his guests would include any beautiful ladies.

Of one thing she was quite certain: the lady who had ordered the Under-Butler to drug his wine would not be present.

Nattie had told her that Hayes had left the house yesterday evening under a cloud.

"I saved him!" Demelza said triumphantly to herself.

She wondered if the Earl was curious as to who had written the note. He would never know, and she found the knowledge somewhat dispiriting.

They arrived back at the Manor and Demelza entered as usual by the garden door so that she should not be seen by any of the Earl's servants who were on duty.

As she went up the secret stairway she could not resist looking into the rooms to see if the flowers she had arranged first thing in the morning before anyone was awake were still looking lovely.

She had cut them from her own garden, which, enclosed by red brick Elizabethan walls, was out of sight of any of the windows of the house.

It was here that her mother had planted an herb-garden, and Demelza took immense trouble in cultivating the same herbs, besides the flowers she loved best.

These included the pink roses she always put in her late father's room.

Climbing over a little arbour at the end of the garden was a riot of honeysuckle intermingled with white roses, which sweetly scented, had been her mother's favourite.

Because she thought the Earl might appreciate them, her bowls of roses in the Drawing-Room were larger than usual and there was hardly a side-table that did not hold them.

She had also changed the roses in his bed-room and thought that they made a perfect splash of colour against the dark panelling.

Then she told herself that as the Earl undoubtedly had so many priceless treasures in his possession he could hardly be expected to concern himself with flowers.

Nevertheless, she took a great deal of trouble over the arrangement on the desk in the Library, where she had realised he wrote his letters and sometimes sat alone first thing in the morning.

She was sure it would be wrong and impolite to spy on him and she had deliberately restricted herself to looking at him in the Dining-Room and of course on the race-course.

There, she could not feel she was intruding, and it was hard to take her eyes from him to the horses.

She kept asking herself why Gerard had said the Earl was so wicked where women were concerned. Perhaps it was because he was so handsome that he excited them to behave as did the lady who had tried to drug him.

She longed to know if he had loved her very much and found herself wondering what happened when a man like the Earl made love to anyone so beautiful.

They would of course kiss each other, and Demelza could not help thinking that that would be a wonderful experience. Yet perhaps she herself would never be kissed.

Nattie was always murmuring that she ought to meet "the right people," and Demelza was well aware that she really meant she should meet eligible bachelors from whom to choose a husband.

"Maybe I shall never marry," she told herself, and thought again how terrible it must be for the Earl to have a wife who was insane.

It gave her almost a physical ache in her heart to think what he must have suffered, and she prayed that such a tragedy would never happen to Gerard.

Walking up the twisting staircase to the Priests'-Room, Demelza decided she would lie down on her bed and read one of the books that she had brought with her into hiding.

The room was so well constructed that it was in fact quite light, although the slit-like windows were close against the low ceiling and hidden under the eaves of the house.

Demelza had cleaned them and the light in the room was diffused and gave the place an air of coolness after the heat of the sun at the races.

She picked up her book but found it hard to concentrate on anything but the races—and the Earl.

He was everything, she thought, that she had always envisaged a man should be: sporting, fond of horses, and, she was quite certain, a magnificent rider.

He seemed to embody all her childhood dreams of St. George, Sir Galahad, and the heroes in Sir Walter Scott's novels, which her father had bought for her each time one was published.

"I never thought then," she whispered, "that I would see the hero of them in real life!"

* * *

Demelza must have fallen asleep, because she awoke with a start to find that there was very little

light in the room, which made her think the sun had
already set.

At that moment she heard Nattie coming clumsily
up the stairs with her evening meal.

Demelza sat up on the bed.

"I have been asleep, Nattie," she said. "What time
is it?"

"Nearly ten o'clock," Nattie answered, "and the
servants are starting their supper."

Demelza almost cried out aloud her disappointment.

She had meant to watch the Earl tonight in the
Dining-Hall. Now it would be too late, and by the
time she had eaten her own food, she was quite certain, they would have moved into the Drawing-Room.

"There was a party tonight," Nattie said almost as
if she knew what Demelza was thinking.

"Were there any ladies present?"

"No, only gentlemen. I expect the conversation was
of nothing but the racing. No-one can think of anything else in this place!"

"And no-one will talk of anything else tomorrow,"
Demelza said with a smile, "when Crusader wins the
Gold Cup."

"*If* he wins!" Nattie said sharply.

"He will!" Demelza replied. "How could the
greatest horse fail to win the greatest race?"

The Ascot Gold Cup had been introduced into
the races in 1807.

The first time it was run it was over two miles, but
it was increased by half a mile the following year.

Demelza had been told that the Queen and the
Princesses had watched the race in a special Pavilion
erected at the arm of the course. Another box had
been completed opposite the judges for the Prince of
Wales.

"Do you remember, Nattie, the very first race for the
Gold Cup?" Demelza asked.

"Of course I remember it!" Nattie replied. "The Queen and the Princesses were wearing mantles in the Spanish style, with what I would call gypsy-hats."

Demelza laughed.

She always teased Nattie about her interest in the Royal Family.

"And who won the race?" Demelza enquired. "That is far more important!"

There was a silence, then Nattie said:

"Believe it or not, Miss Demelza, it's slipped my memory!"

Demelza laughed again.

"You were watching the Queen instead of Master Jackey!"

"Perhaps I found Her Majesty more interesting," Nattie retorted almost defiantly.

"Well, you can forget the King tomorrow and concentrate on Crusader!" Demelza said. "I do not suppose the prize money of one hundred guineas will be of importance to the Earl. It will be the honour and the glory which count."

She was thinking of how every year owners and jockeys strove to win what had originally been called "the Emperor's Place" because besides the prize-money there was a gift of plate presented by the Tsar of Russia, Nicholas I.

Demelza's father had always been more interested in the Gold Cup than any other race and he had inspired her with his own enthusiasm.

Nattie's mind was, however, still on the Royal Personages she had seen in the past, and she was relating how King George III and his suite used to arrive on horseback, when as if suddenly she realised the time she rose to pick up Demelza's tray, saying:

"Now you go to bed, Miss Demelza. If you're not tired you ought to be!"

"I was tired when I first came home," Demelza

admitted, "but now, as I told you, I have been asleep and feel very wakeful."

"Then don't strain your eyes trying to read until all hours of the night," Nattie admonished.

She had always been convinced that candlelight was too dim for reading and Demelza had heard her say the same thing over and over again during the years when she had been growing up.

"Good-night, dearest Nattie," she said, "and do not worry about me. Remember, I want my very best gown to wear tomorrow."

That could only be another white muslin, but it was new, and, unlike Demelza's other gowns, it was trimmed with some pretty ribbons which had seemed both to her and to Nattie a vast expenditure when they had bought them.

Alone, Demelza undressed and put on her night-gown and over it a white dressing-gown also made by Nattie. It fastened close at the neck and had a little flat collar trimmed with lace.

She brushed her hair as her mother had taught her to do until it shone; then, still feeling wide awake, she picked up her book and forced herself to concentrate on it.

Before she did so she lit two candles, which Nattie would have thought, eyes or no eyes, an extravagance.

Then because her book had begun to interest her she forgot everything else until with surprise she heard the stable-clock strike the hour of midnight.

"I certainly must go to sleep now," she told herself, and shut her book to put it away tidily.

Everything in the Priests'-Room had to be put back in place because it was so small.

Then as she stretched her arms above her head, feeling a little cramped after sitting for so long, Demelza had a sudden longing to breathe the fresh air.

One disadvantage of the Priests'-Room was that it was not well ventilated, and for the first time since she had slept there Demelza felt stifled and restricted.

'I will go downstairs and stand at the garden door,' she thought. "I will breathe deeply, then come up again. Not even Nattie could find fault with that!'

She slipped her feet into her soft satin heel-less slippers and very quietly began to descend the stairs.

She passed the top floor, reached the first, and was just proceeding farther when she heard voices in what was known as the Red Room.

Someone was speaking clearly but in what seemed a deliberately lowered tone and there was something almost sinister about it, as if the words were hissed.

Without actually realising that she would be prying on the occupant's privacy, Demelza stopped and standing on tip-toe looked through the small hole which was incorporated in the Jacobean panelling with which the room was lined.

As she did so she remembered that it was Sir Francis Wigdon who slept there, the man she disliked.

She could see him sitting on the side of the bed. He was still wearing his evening-clothes but had loosened the cravat round his neck.

"You have brought exactly what I told you?" Demelza heard him say in a lowered voice, which made his words seem deliberately secretive.

She moved slightly so that she could see to whom he was speaking and saw to her surprise that there were two other men in the room.

One looked like a valet, wearing a striped waistcoat in what she thought were Sir Francis's colours. The other was a much rougher type, coarse and wearing a red handkerchief round his neck.

He held his cap in his hands, which he was twisting nervously as he said:

"Oi've got it safe, Guv'nor."

"You are sure it is strong enough to be effective?" Sir Francis asked, speaking now to the man who appeared to be his valet.

"I can swear, Sir, that when 'e's taken it Crusader'll not run tomorrow."

"Good!" Sir Francis ejaculated.

Demelza held her breath as if she could not believe what she had heard.

"Then get on with you!" Sir Francis ordered. "But be absolutely certain before you enter the stables that everyone is asleep."

"We'll be cautious, Sir," the valet replied.

Demelza did not wait to hear any more. She knew now what the men intended to do.

There had always been talk of horses being doped before races, and of owners having guards to watch their stables. But she was quite certain it had never crossed the Earl's mind, or Abbot's, that the horses were not safe at the Manor.

Her first thought was that she must wake Gerard, but it was impossible to get directly into his room and she was afraid if she went into the corridor she might encounter the men to whom Sir Francis was speaking, or even Sir Francis himself.

Almost without conscious thought her feet carried her along the side-passage which led to the Master's Room.

Only as she descended the steps which led to the secret panel by the fireplace did she ask herself if she was doing the right thing and she remembered how furious Gerard would be with her.

Then she told herself that nothing mattered but that she should save Crusader.

How could she stand by and do nothing while he was doped and made unfit to race the following day?

It was not only that the Earl would lose face at having to withdraw his horse and that he and Gerard would lose the money they had wagered on him. It was also a humiliation and an ignominy that such things should happen at the Manor of all places.

She put out her hand without even waiting to look through the peep-hole.

The secret door opened and she stepped into the room which had been her father's.

The curtains were drawn back and by the light of the stars and a pale moon that was creeping up the sky she could see clearly enough to realise that the Earl was in bed and asleep.

Drawing a deep breath, Demelza spoke. . . .

*   *   *

The Earl had enjoyed his dinner when the house-party had been joined by six of his closest friends.

The food had been excellent, the wine superb, and although the conversation had naturally been about the racing, everyone told amusing anecdotes of one sort or another.

They capped one another's jokes with a wit that made the Earl feel sorry that the King was not present.

If there was the one thing that George IV really enjoyed it was witty conversation to which he could contribute with an intelligence that few people except his closest friends credited him with.

"A damned good evening, Valient!" one of the Earl's guests said when he left. "I cannot remember when I have laughed more."

As the Earl went up to bed he thought he had been wise in insisting that everyone should retire early.

Like the King, he hated parties that went on too long and he disliked it if men drank so much that they became incoherent.

Abstemious himself, he found drunkards a bore and he never allowed himself to be bored.

When he got into bed he echoed the sentiments of Lord Chirn, who had said as they walked upstairs together:

"This is the best Ascot I have ever attended, Valient. Not only have I made money, but I have never been more comfortable and I find in the peace and quiet of this house that I sleep like a child."

It was what the Earl had found.

There were no noisy chambermaids or whistling ostlers to wake him in the morning, and the clean air coming in through the windows carried the scent of the pines and flowers.

He fell asleep almost as soon as his head touched the pillow. Then he awoke with an alertness which came from his training as a soldier.

It was almost as if he sensed danger before he heard a very soft voice say:

"Go to Crusader! Go to Crusader!"

He turned towards the sound and incredulously saw the ghost of the White Lady!

It was the same vision he had seen when he arrived in the Long Gallery, and here she was again, standing by the fireplace. He could see her quite clearly in the light from the window.

Then as he moved to sit up she said again:

"Go to Crusader! Go now! It is urgent!"

The Earl sat up completely and as he did so the White Lady vanished!

One moment she was there, the next she was gone and there was only the outline of the mantelpiece against the darkness of the panelling.

"I am dreaming," the Earl told himself.

But he was awake, and because of the urgency in the soft voice he knew he must do what he had been told, if only to make sure that the whole thing was nothing but imagination.

He got out of bed, and pulled on a shirt and a pair

of close-fitting pantaloons with a speed which would have annoyed Dawson, who liked to dress his Master slowly.

He shrugged himself into the first coat he took from the wardrobe and tied a cravat loosely round his neck. Then with his feet in a pair of soft-soled slippers he opened the door and walked down the corridor.

The house was in darkness except for one candle which had been left burning in the hall in a silver candlestick.

The Earl picked it up and it lit him along a corridor which led, he knew, towards the stables.

Only when he reached a side-door before the kitchen-quarters did he set the candle down on a table, undo the bolts, and let himself out.

As he felt the coldness of the night air on his face he told himself that he was being a fool to pay any attention to what had undoubtedly been a very vivid dream.

Yet, if, as he expected, he found Crusader safe and undisturbed, he could just make his way back to bed and no-one would know that he had been seeing visions or whatever one might call them.

'I expect the wine was stronger than I thought, and because I was thirsty I drank too much of it,' the Earl decided.

At the same time, the White Lady had seemed very real. If she was a ghost—did ghosts speak?

He decided he was lamentably ignorant on the subject. Then as he rounded the huge overgrown laurels and had his first sight of the stables, he saw something ahead of him move.

Instinctively he stood still.

The movement he had seen was in the shadow at the entrance to the stables. Once again he thought he was imagining things, until the movement occurred again.

Now he realised that it was a hand, and a hand must belong to a person.

He waited.

A few seconds later he discerned two men moving stealthily in a manner which proclaimed all too clearly that they were up to mischief, creeping towards the stable.

They kept in the shadow of the building and the Earl knew that his warning from the White Lady had only just come in time.

He remembered now that his groom had mentioned that the lock to the main stable door at the Manor was broken.

The Earl had hardly listened at the time. It had not seemed to be of any importance.

The grooms would doubtless be sleeping over the stables as they always did, but, apart from anything else, since his plans had been changed at the last moment it was unlikely that any of the unsavoury characters on the race-course would know where he was staying.

One man ahead of the other pulled open the stable door, then as they disappeared inside the Earl moved.

His slippers made no sound on the cobbled yard and when he entered the stable like a whirlwind they were at Crusader's stall, undoing the iron gate.

He caught the first man who turned round to look at him a blow on the chin which lifted his feet off the ground.

The other man, bigger and more aggressive, went for him, but the Earl had learnt the art of boxing from the greatest professional pugilists of his generation, "Gentleman Jackson" and his partner Mendoza.

It was nothing of a fight, for his opponent was laid out and unconscious within a few seconds.

It was then that the Earl shouted and the grooms

came running, with them Baxter, his Head Groom, and old Abbot.

They searched the unconscious men and found the drug with which they had intended to dope Crusader, and as Baxter held it out in the palm of his hand towards the Earl he said:

"I apologise, M'Lord. I should've left a guard on th' 'orses, but I thinks we were safe enough 'ere."

"We have learnt a lesson we will not forget in the future, Baxter," the Earl said. "I wonder who paid these thugs."

As he spoke, Abbot, who was holding the lantern over the smaller man, gave an exclamation.

"What is it?" the Earl enquired.

"Oi've seen this man afore, M'Lord. 'E's visited th' stables several times since 'e's been a-staying at th' Manor."

"Staying at the Manor?" the Earl asked sharply.

"Aye, M'Lord. 'E tells Oi 'e were interested in 'orses, especially Crusader."

"Who is he?" the Earl enquired.

" 'E says 'e were a valet, M'Lord. And 'e's a-wearing a livery waist-coat."

The Earl looked down. By the light of the lantern he could see the buttons that fastened the striped waistcoat and he recognised the crest on them.

"Tie this vermin up," he said to Baxter. "Lock them up for the night, and I will see they are handed over to the race-course Police in the morning."

"Very good, M'Lord, an' thank ye, M'Lord. I can only say how humiliated I am that this should've occurred."

"Fortunately I was warned in time," the Earl remarked.

"Warned, M'Lord?"

It was a question which, the Earl thought as he walked back to the house, he could not answer.

He walked upstairs and without knocking opened the door of the Red Room.

Sir Francis was half-undressed and not in bed.

The expression on his face as the Earl entered was one both of fear and guilt.

"I give you ten minutes in which to get out of this house!" the Earl said curtly.

"What is . . ." Sir Francis began, only to be silenced as the Earl interrupted:

"If you are wise, you will leave the country. Your accomplices will doubtless betray you to the Police, and a warrant will be issued for your arrest."

Sir Francis was silent.

Just for a moment the Earl was tempted to knock him down, then he decided that it would be beneath his dignity.

"Ten minutes!" he repeated and went from the room closing the door behind him.

As he reached his own bed-room the full force of what had happened made him stare incredulously at the place where he had seen the White Lady speaking to him.

He walked towards it and as he did so was aware of that sweet elusive perfume and knew who it was who had left him the note warning him not to drink the wine.

"First me, then my horse," the Earl said with a twist of his lips.

Ghosts did not write letters even if, incredibly, they were able to speak.

He stood staring at where he had seen the White Lady. Then he put out his hand and began to feel the panelling. . . .

Far away in the depths of his memory he recalled when he was a small boy staying with his parents at a house in Worcestershire.

It had been very old and surrounded by a moat, which had delighted him.

His parents had paid little attention to him and as there were no other children in the house he had attached himself to the Curator.

He had been a kindly man who had shown him the pictures of battles and other dramatic events in history with which the house abounded.

Then, because he had been an intelligent little boy, the Curator had told him the story of the Battle of Worcester and how the fugitive King had hidden in an oak tree to escape those pursuing him.

"Some of his followers hid here in this house," the Curator went on.

He had then shown the Earl the secret passage where the Royalists remained undiscovered by the Cromwellian soldiers.

To reach it, the Earl remembered, there had been a panel which opened in the wall just wide enough to allow a man to pass through it.

He thought that the Curator had pressed a certain spot in the carving and could remember seeing his fingers feeling for it. Then he remembered his excitement when the panelling opened.

Now his own fingers were feeling among the leaves, the scrolls, the exquisitely carved heads of corn, then the flowers.

He was just beginning to believe that his search would prove unsuccessful when he found what he sought!

As he pressed, a door in the panelling opened and he saw surprisingly on the other side of it there were two pairs of riding-boots!

The Earl went back into his bed-room and lit the candle that stood beside his bed in a brass candlestick.

Then, holding it high to light his way, he went

through the panelling, feeling that he was starting on a voyage of discovery as exciting as anything he had ever done in his life before.

Very softly and moving slowly so as not to make a noise, the Earl climbed the narrow, twisting staircase.

Occasionally he stopped to look at where it branched off into other passages, but he continued climbing all the time until he saw a light ahead of him and was aware that he had almost reached the top of the house.

A second or two later he found what he sought.

The Priests'-Room was very small and he saw that it contained a couch against one wall and on the other there was a picture of the Madonna encircled with flowers.

Below it jutting out from the wall itself was what was little more than a shelf but had obviously in the past been used as an altar by the hunted Priests to say Mass.

On the narrow altar now were two lighted candles and between them a bowl of white roses.

Kneeling in front of it with her hands pressed palm to palm in the eternal attitude of a woman in prayer was the White Lady.

Her hair, which fell over her shoulders, was so pale in the light from the candles that it seemed almost silver.

The Earl could see that she was little and slender enough to be a child, but the white robe which buttoned down the front revealed the soft curve of her breasts.

She was in profile and her small nose was straight and aristocratic, her lashes dark against her pale cheeks.

It was a long time since the Earl had last seen a woman kneeling in prayer and it certainly was not what he had expected to find as he climbed the stairs.

Then as if she were aware instinctively that she was

not alone, the woman he was watching turned her head.

The Earl found himself looking into the largest and strangest eyes he had ever seen, which seemed to fill the whole of her small face.

For a moment she was very still. Then quietly in the voice which had spoken to him in his bed-room she said:

"Crusader?"

It was a question.

"He is safe!" the Earl answered. "I went to him as you told me to do."

She gave a sigh of relief which seemed to come from the very depths of her being.

"You were praying for him?" the Earl asked.

"Yes. I was afraid . . . terribly afraid . . . you would be too . . . late."

"Your prayers were answered."

Then as she rose slowly to her feet the Earl asked:

"Who are you? I thought you were a ghost!"

She smiled and it seemed to transform the expression on her face from one of perfect spirituality to something very human, and yet in its own way equally lovely.

"The White Lady," she said. "That is who I hoped . . . you would think I was when you . . . saw me in the . . . Long Gallery."

"Why? Why do you have to hide yourself," the Earl asked.

He had a strange feeling that he had walked into another world. Despite her smile and the fact that they were talking to each other, he felt she was not real, but as ethereal as the ghost she had pretended to be.

"What . . . happened to . . . Crusader?" she replied, as if her thoughts were still on the horse.

"There were two men attempting to dope him," the Earl replied. "I knocked them out. They are still unconscious."

"I hoped ... you would do ... that."

There was no mistaking the admiration in her strange eyes, which seemed to the Earl to be almost purple, although he was sure he must be mistaken.

She looked down at his hand and gave an exclamation.

"You are bleeding!"

For the first time the Earl realised that he had broken the skin on his knuckles with the force with which he had struck first the valet and then the larger man, who had not gone down at the first punch.

"It is nothing," he said.

"But it is!" Demelza insisted. "It might become septic and would then be very painful."

She opened a cupboard in the wall and took out from it a small china basin and a ewer in the same patterned china.

She set it down on a chair, then brought a linen towel from the cupboard and with it a little box.

The Earl stood watching her, seeming unnaturally large and broad-shouldered in the confines of the small room, until she said:

"I think My Lord, you had better sit down on the bed so that I can treat your hand properly."

The Earl was too intrigued to do anything but obey.

He put his lighted candle down beside the others on the altar and sat down.

Demelza went down on her knees beside him before she poured some water from the ewer into the basin; then, opening the box, she added what the Earl realised were herbs.

"What is your name?" he asked as she stirred the water with her fingers.

"Demelza."

"Cornish!"

"My mother came from Cornwall."

"As I do."

"But of course!" she exclaimed. "I had forgotten that Trevarnon is a Cornish name . . . but I might have . . . guessed."

"Are you Gerard Langston's sister?"

She nodded as she took his hand in both of hers, dipped it into the cold water, and washed it very carefully.

He wondered if any other woman would have touched him so impersonally, but Demelza was completely unselfconscious while he was vividly conscious of her.

"Do you grow the herbs in the small garden which is surrounded by the red brick walls?" he asked.

"It was Mama's herb-garden."

He gave a sudden exclamation.

"Honeysuckle!"

She looked up at him in surprise and he said:

"The scent you use, which has been haunting me —I can smell it now on your hair."

"It is the honeysuckle which grows over the arbour in the herb-garden. Mama taught me how to distill the oil from the flowers in the spring."

"I could not put a name to it," the Earl explained, "although I was conscious of it everywhere in the house and especially on the note you left for me."

"I did not . . . know how else to . . . warn you."

"How did you know that the wine would drug me?"

He saw the flush of colour on Demelza's cheeks, and before she could reply he exclaimed:

"But of course! You can see into the rooms!"

"I only looked . . . occasionally," Demelza said. "I was . . . surprised to hear a lady speaking in the . . . Drawing-Room when I came back from the . . . races, and tonight I was going . . . downstairs because it was so hot in here and I wanted to breathe the . . . fresh air."

"And you heard Sir Francis speaking?" the Earl prompted.

"I heard him speaking in a ... strange voice that sounded somehow secretive and ... sinister. I have not ... listened or looked at other times, except the first night when ... you were in the ... Dining-Room."

She glanced up at him, hoping he would understand, and he said slowly:

"You heard me asking your brother about the White Lady?"

"Yes ... I was in the ... Ministrels' Gallery."

"Perhaps I was subconsciously aware of your presence there, but I was already intrigued as to how someone could vanish so completely in the Long Gallery unless they were a ghost."

As if the words recalled to Demelza how angry Gerard would be at her having met the Earl, she rose to go once again to the cupboard. She came back with a piece of linen which she tore into strips.

"I am going to put this round your hand to keep it clean for tonight," she said, "and then please ... will you ... forget that you ... have met ... me?"

"Why?" the Earl asked.

"Because Gerard made me promise that I would not ... come into the ... house while ... you were here. Unless I ... promised, he said I must go away ... but I had nowhere to go."

"Have you any idea why your brother was so insistent that we should not meet?" the Earl asked.

He knew the answer by the way Demelza dropped her eyes, and again there was a blush against the fairness of her skin.

"Your brother was quite right," he said. "We will keep our meeting a secret, although I shall find it hard to explain how I managed to save Crusader."

"You might just have felt intuitively that something was wrong," Demelza said quickly. "I would not ...

wish you to ... lie, but Gerard would be so very ...
angry with ... me."

"I see he has made me out to be a monster!" the
Earl answered in an angry voice.

"Gerard admires you very ... much, as does ...
everyone else," Demelza said. "It is just ..."

"Just my unsavoury reputation where women are
concerned," the Earl finished.

There was no need for her to confirm that that was
the truth.

"Because I am so grateful to you," he said, "for saving me and for saving Crusader, I will keep the fact
that you and I have met a secret."

"That is ... kind of you. I would not ... wish Gerard to ... worry, which he ... will do."

"He shall remain in blissful ignorance of everything
that has occurred," the Earl promised.

He rose from the bed and, putting out his unband-
aged hand, took Demelza's in his.

"Thank you!" he said. "Thank you, my little
White Lady, for all have done for me. If Crusader
wins tomorrow, the victory will be yours."

He kissed her hand.

Picking up his candle, he took one last look at the
strange pansy-coloured eyes raised to his. Then slowly
he descended the narrow stairs.

Chapter Five

Sitting at the glittering gold-ornamented table at Windsor Castle, the Earl found it extremely difficult to concentrate on what was being said.

He had received the congratulations of everyone present, and he had in fact felt they were well deserved.

Crusader had won the Gold Cup, beating Sir Huldibrand after one of the finest and closest races ever seen at Ascot.

Sir Huldibrand had made the first running at a brisk rate as far as the dog kennels, then Crusader came in front and made the fastest pace down the hill.

At the turn of the course Crusader and Sir Huldibrand were neck to neck together, and, as the Earl heard someone say beside him: "It is a toss-up who would be the winner."

Then there was a tremendous, slashing struggle between the two magnificent horses, which ended with Crusader passing the winning-post first by a nose.

"I have never seen a better race, Valient!" the King had said to the Earl when it was over. "But we might have guessed that as usual your persistent luck would enable you to carry off the highest trophy of the meet-ing."

He gave a little sigh because, although it had been expected, his own horse had been unplaced.

But, being genuinely fond of the Earl, he had drunk his health not once but several times during the dinner at which the winner of the Gold Cup was always the Guest of Honour.

The Earl was aware that Lady Sydel was gazing at him across the table with an expression that he could not help thinking had something murderous about it!

Then he laughed to himself for being overly dra-matic and was determined that he had no intention, however hard she might manoeuvre, of talking with her alone.

All through the race-meeting he found himself searching the crowd with his field-glasses for a face with huge pansy-coloured eyes and wearing what he was sure would be a white gown.

But it was impossible to distinguish anyone in the seething mob, which was greater for the Gold Cup than on any other day of the week.

All along the course for nearly a mile were ranged lines of carriages, and in front of them stood the spec-tators who had been temporarily driven from the track, which they used as a promenade between the races.

In some places the carriages were ten deep and it was almost impossible for those at the back to have any chance of seeing the race.

Because of the fine weather, and perhaps because everyone expected a fighting finish between the two horses on which an enormous amount of money had been wagered, it was more difficult than usual to clear the course.

Originally, the Earl remembered, this was the duty of the Yeoman Pickers, but they had been succeeded by mounted patrols of Police.

The difficulty in getting everything ready for the actual race usually resulted, as it had this afternoon, in their running late.

After he had changed his clothes at the Manor, the Earl had therefore been obliged to travel to the Castle at a speed which made Jem, who accompanied him, occasionally draw in his breath apprenhensively.

However, they arrived without mishap, although they learnt later that there had been a number of accidents on the road to London in which at least two people had lost their lives and several horses had been badly injured.

The King, despite his gout, was in good spirits, and the Earl thought whatever the criticism regarding Lady Conyngham, she was an attractive woman and made His Majesty happy.

The Earl found that everyone in the Royal Party and the extra guests invited for the occasion were all close friends.

He had always been extremely fond of the Duke of York, who had enjoyed an excellent Ascot and was also receiving congratulations on his wins.

"It is my best-ever race-meeting," he told the Earl sleepily, "and my horses have won me something handsome in the way of bets!"

The Duke of York was not clever, but he had an understanding of people which enabled him to avoid the errors into which his brothers had fallen, making them both unpopular and contemptible.

He was in fact both respected and loved, and the Earl on many occasions had said confidentially to his friends:

"His Royal Highness is the only one of the Princes who has the feelings and behaviour of an English gentleman."

At dinner the Earl had the attractive Princess Esterhazy on his left, who was only too willing to flirt with him as she had done so often on previous occasions.

But this evening he kept thinking of his strange adventure of the night before, and the picture of Demelza kneeling in the Priests'-Room in front of the altar kept intruding on his mind when he least expected it.

He had a sudden, urgent desire to be back in the quietness and mystery of the Manor and to open once again the secret door in the panelling of his bed-room.

It was so insistent that when the King retired immediately after dinner was over, saying that he was fatigued after the races and his gout was painful, the Earl went with him.

He did not say good-bye to anyone, knowing that if he did so he would be detained for a long time.

Instead he followed the King to the door, and as if His Majesty realised what he was doing he good-humouredly took him by the arm and drew him outside the Salon, leaning on him as they walked down the corridor.

"You cannot really intend to leave so soon, Valient?" he said.

"A party loses its savour when you are not there, Sire," the Earl replied flatteringly.

"What you mean is, there are other attractions elsewhere," the King remarked with a twinkle in his eye.

The Earl did not reply and His Majesty continued:

"Lady Sydel asked me to intercede with you on her behalf. I gather she craves your forgiveness."

"How unfortunate, Sire," the Earl replied, "that you did not have an opportunity to speak intimately with me."

The King chuckled.

"Up to your old tricks, Valient? No woman likes being a 'has-been.'"

The Earl thought that perhaps His Majesty was remembering how bitterly Mrs. Fitzherbert had complained when he discarded her for Lady Hertford. So, aloud he said:

"I know I can always rely on your understanding, Sire, and your vast knowledge of feminine vagaries."

The King was delighted, as the Earl knew he would be.

"I do understand, Valient," he said. "But if you take my advice you will move quickly under cover before the hounds are on your scent."

He laughed at his own joke, clapped the Earl on the back, and went to his private apartments.

This enabled his guest to hurry down the stairs, call his Phaeton, and be away from the Castle before the rest of the party had any idea that he had left.

Driving back to the Manor, the Earl was determined that he would see Demelza again and talk to her.

Everything about her intrigued him and he told himself he had never known a woman with such a spiritual and unusual beauty.

He wondered what she would look like in the daytime and was half-afraid that he might be disappointed.

Could her eyes really be the pansy shade he had thought them to be last night? Had she really a grace that was different from other women?

He remembered the softness of her hands as she had touched his and the manner in which she had bandaged him without being in the least self-conscious that he was sitting on her bed and they were alone.

He did not know any other woman who would have behaved in the same way in such circumstances.

'She is only a child,' he thought to himself.

Yet there had been a budding maturity in the lovely curves of her body, and he thought too that she was intelligent, as he had not expected a young girl to be.

'I must see her,' he vowed, 'although of course on second acquaintance I may be disappointed.'

It was as if he was being cynical merely to safeguard himself.

He knew that it was not only Demelza that he was finding so intriguing but her background: the beauty and mystery of the Manor, the secret staircase, and of course the way she had saved both him and Crusader.

"She will expect me this evening," he said aloud, remembering that he had told her that if Crusader won the Gold Cup the victory was hers.

It was only a little after ten o'clock when he reached the Manor, and because he had no desire to become involved with his guests who he knew were having a party, he drove not to the front door but directly into the stables.

His grooms came running to the horses' head. He stepped down and only pausing to congratulate Baxter once again on a very successful day, entered the house by the side-door he had used the previous night.

When he was in the passage he could hear laughter and voices coming from the Dining-Hall and realised that the party was in full swing and doubtless the port was being passed round the table continuously.

He moved quickly up the secondary staircase which took him to the passage on which his bed-room opened.

He guessed that Dawson, not expecting him home so early, would be downstairs having his meal, and in fact in his bed-room the candles were not yet lit.

There was, however, still a faint glow in the sky from the sun, which had set in a burst of golden glory behind the Manor.

The stars were coming out faintly overhead and there was a pale bit of the moon to be seen, which the Earl knew once it was fully risen would with its silver light make the Manor seem more enchanted than it appeared already.

He stood for a moment in his bed-room, smelling the fragrance of the roses and seeking the scent of honeysuckle.

He thought it would tell him whether Demelza had come through the secret door today, if, as another woman would have done, she had wanted to look at where he slept and touch the things he had used.

But somehow disappointingly the perfume of honey-suckle was not discernible.

Shutting the door into the passage quietly, the Earl walked across the room to grope as he had done the night before amongst the carving for the secret catch which would open the way to the twisting stairs.

He found it, and pressed, but nothing happened!

He thought he must have been mistaken. He pressed again, but still the oak panel remained immobile.

For a moment he wondered if something had gone wrong and the catch had ceased to function. Then he was aware that the door had been barred.

Never, in all the years in which he had pursued women, or rather they had pursued him, could the Earl remember any other occasion when a door had been closed against him.

In fact usually they were opened before he reached them and the occupant was in his arms without waiting for an invitation.

Perplexed, the Earl stood looking at the panelling as if he could hardly credit that he had in fact been locked out.

Then he told himself that it was a challenge, which was something he had never refused.

At the same time, he wondered helplessly what he could do about it.

He could hardly knock on wood, and even if he did, it was doubtful that Demelza would hear it at the top of the house.

He thought with a sudden feeling of despair that he

had no other access to the secret staircase which led to the Priests'-Room.

He remembered that Demelza had said she had watched him from the Minstrel's Gallery. That meant that there was an entrance there, but he could hardly go blundering about in the Gallery with his party sitting beneath him, where they might hear his movements.

The Earl was well aware that he had been fortunate last night in finding the secret catch merely because he had seen Demelza standing in his room.

Whoever had designed the labyrinth of passages and entrances had done so to save men's lives and make the hiding-place almost impregnable unless they were betrayed.

In his bed-room the secret panel opened beside the fireplace, but he was quite certain that in other rooms its position would be very different.

How then could he spend hours, perhaps days or weeks, searching for another entrance in a house in which, he had already noticed, almost every room was panelled?

'What can I do?' he wondered to himself.

Now his desire to see Demelza was increased a thousandfold simply because she was elusive.

"I *have* to see her! I *will* see her!" he said aloud, and swore beneath his breath that he would not be defeated.

Without consciously realising what he was doing, since he was concentrating so completely on the problem which beset him, he opened the door of his bedroom and walked slowly and thoughtfully down the corridor.

He was in fact working out how the house was constructed and trying to guess where the walls were most likely to be wide enough to contain a passage.

At the same time, he wanted to co-ordinate it with

the route he had taken last night when he had climbed to the very top of the building.

He had seen Demelza first in the Long Gallery, but that was at an angle to the centre part of the house.

He did not seem to be getting very far with his calculations when at the far end of the passage beyond the main staircase he saw a figure carrying a tray.

He recognised Nattie and knew that she had come up a third staircase from the kitchens which lay beyond the stairs he had used himself.

Nattie turned left and walked away from him. Alert and interested the Earl followed her at a respectful distance keeping to the side of the corridor.

The candles had not yet been lit and the passage was in fact almost in darkness. He was half-afraid that Nattie would disappear and he would lose her as he had lost the White Lady in the Long Gallery.

Then she stopped, and, balancing her tray with one hand, she opened a door with the other.

She disappeared inside and the Earl quickened his pace and walked hurriedly to the door, which Nattie, having passed through, had pushed to with her foot.

But it was not completely closed, and opening it just a fraction so that he could look inside, the Earl had a glimpse of the Nurse disappearing through a panel in the wall on the other side of the room.

The curtains were not drawn over the windows and there was enough light for him to see that the room was not in use. There were holland covers on the bed, the chairs, and over the dressing-table.

The Earl realised that luck was with him, and he held his breath, for he saw that although Nattie had entered the secret passage she had not, because she was encumbered with the tray, shut the panel behind her.

Quickly he entered the room and crossed to the opposite wall.

Hearing Nattie's footsteps moving rather heavily upwards, he waited for a few seconds, then swiftly and silently he entered through the dark aperture. Inside, he moved down the stairs until he thought that he would be out of sight when Nattie returned.

He heard a faint murmur of voices far away; then, leaning against the wall in the darkness, he told himself that once again his winning streak had not failed him.

* * *

"I'm sorry to be late, dearie," Nattie said as she entered the Priests'-Room.

"I expected it," Demelza answered, rising to take the tray from her.

"It's always the same when there's a big party and more courses than usual," Nattie said. "The servants have to wait for their meal and so do you."

"It has given me a good appetite," Demelza said with a smile.

"I chose the dishes I thought you'd like best," Nattie said.

"They look delicious!" Demelza cried. "But whatever they were like I would not be particular."

She had been far too excited at the races to eat the sandwiches and small pasties which Nattie had brought for luncheon or even a delicious mousse which Betsy had purloined from the kitchen when the Chef was not looking.

All Demelza had been able to think about was Crusader and pray that he would not be beaten by Sir Huldibrand even though she knew Mr. Ramsbottom's horse was a worthy rival.

When finally Crusader had passed the winning-post and a great cheer of excitement had gone up, she had felt the tears prick her eyes at the intensity of her joy.

If she had not overheard the plot against him, the horse might have been lying doped and helpless in his stall, and Sir Francis, who would have backed Sir Huldibrand to win, would have been in possession of an illicit fortune.

"There were some strange goings-on last night, Miss Demelza," Nattie had told her early that morning.

"What has happened?" Demelza had asked.

"Two men attempted to drug Crusader," Nattie related, "but His Lordship heard them, and, Abbot said, laid them out like a professional boxer!"

"What a terrible thing to have occurred here in our own stables!" Demelza exclaimed.

"Disgraceful!" Nattie agreed. "The criminals have been taken away by the race-course Police and one of His Lordship's guests has left in a great hurry."

"Who was that?" Demelza asked, knowing she was expected to be curious.

"Sir Francis Wigdon," Nattie answered. "One can hardly believe that a gentleman and a friend of His Lordship's would be mixed up in anything so disreputable."

"No, indeed," Demelza murmured.

On the way to the race-course Abbot could talk of nothing else.

" 'Tis my fault, Miss Demelza," he reproached himself. "Oi should've 'ad that lock on th' stable door mended a time ago, but what do we usually keep in 'em which'd attract th' attention of felons?"

"We must be more careful in the future, Abbot," Demelza replied. "Supposing someone tried to prevent Firebird from running on Saturday?"

"Anyone as tries'll do so over me dead body!" Abbot swore.

Then he chuckled.

" 'Tis just like His Lordship's luck to 'ave an instinct which saved Crusader for th' race."

"Was it an instinct?" Demelza enquired.

"That's what Mr. Dawson, his valet, tells Oi it were."

Demelza smiled secretly to herself, thinking that she had suggested that was what the Earl should say.

"His Lordship's certainly a very fortunate man," Nattie interposed.

"Aye, since 'e's been full grown," Abbot replied. "But Mr. Dawson were a-telling Oi that th' old Earl were a regular tyrant an' 'is son, like everyone else, suffered 'cause o' it."

"A tyrant?" Demelza asked with interest. "In what way?"

"Mr. Dawson said everyone in 'is Lordship's employment went in fear of 'is rages and neither 'e nor 'er Ladyship took any interest in their son."

"They neglected him?" Demelza enquired.

"Ignored 'im, more like," Abbot replied. "Ye be lucky, Miss Demelza, in havin' a father and mother what fair doted on ye. A number of th' gentry an' th' nobility 'as no use for their children."

"That's true enough," Nattie agreed. "They put them in the care of ignorant and neglectful servants, and I've heard of cases where the poor little creatures are half-starved!"

Demelza was silent.

It semed extraordinary that the Earl, who was so wealthy, envied by his contemporaries for his vast possessions, and who appeared to be the most fortunate man alive, should have suffered as a child.

True or not, she was sure that because like her he had no brothers or sisters, he must often have felt lonely.

Without having loving parents, what would her life have been like? She could hardly visualise it.

At the same time, whatever she might feel about

him, however much she might commiserate because he
had suffered when he was a child and because of the
tragedy of his marriage, she knew that she must not
see him again.

The circumstances which had led her first to save
him from the vengeance of Lady Sydel and then to
protect Crusader were so exceptional that her disobe-
dience of Gerard's orders and her broken promise to
him were excusable.

Now, although she longed to talk to the Earl, to
watch him as she had done before, she knew she must
behave as her mother would have expected her to do.

It was what she herself knew to be right.

Accordingly, when they returned from the races she
had put the bolt across the secret door which led to
the Earl's bed-room.

She had then gone quickly upstairs, determined
that she would not go down them again until the
morning, in case she should overhear anything else
which was not intended for her ears.

It had, however, been impossible not to think about
the Earl.

When she had seen him leading Crusader to the
weighing room after the race was over she thought
that no other man or horse could equal them in the
whole length and breadth of the country.

She had thrilled to hear the cheers that accompanied
them.

Although a number of people must have lost a lot
of money on the race, as sportsmen they cheered the
victor because he had run a brilliant race in the finest
traditions of the Turf.

"Thank you for a very good dinner," Demelza said
to Nattie now.

She put down her spoon and fork and poured out
a little lemonade from the glass jug on the tray.

"I wish I could tell the Chef how much I appreciate his cooking," she went on.

"That's one thing you can't do," Nattie said. "And if you want the truth, Miss Demelza, I'll be glad when you can come out of this stuffy little hole and go back to your own room."

"After His Lordship and his party have left," Demelza said in a low voice.

"That's right!" Nattie agreed. "I feel as if they'd stayed here for a month already!"

"Has it been a great deal of extra work for you?" Demelza asked.

"It's not the work I mind," Nattie replied. "It's all this being on my guard against anyone learning that you're in the house. Old Betsy almost gave the game away this very morning. Then she catches my eye and bites back the words, but I were only just in time."

"Never mind, Nattie. It is only for another two days," Demelza said.

As she spoke she felt as if her own voice sounded dull and dismal at the thought.

When the horses had gone and the Earl with them, how would she ever settle down? How would she ever be content with the quiet, uneventful life she had known before?

"I'll be getting back," Nattie was saying. "Now don't stay up all night reading. If you ask me, you've had enough excitement for one day!"

"It has certainly been exciting!" Demelza agreed. "Good-night, dearest Nattie!"

She kissed her Nurse's cheek and lifted one of the lighted candles so that the old woman could see her way more clearly down the narrow stairway.

She held it until she saw Nattie move through the panelled door and heard it close behind her.

Then she carried the candle to the altar and set it

down to stand looking up at the Holy picture she had
known ever since she had been a child.

"Thank you, God," she said. "Thank you for letting
him win."

She was sure it was her prayers that not only had
saved Crusader but had carried him first past the
winning-post. Her mother had always said that one
should never receive an answer to a prayer without
being grateful for it.

"Thank you! Thank you!" Demelza said again.

As her lips moved she was seeing not only Crusader
but the Earl walking beside him, with a smile on his
lips as he raised his hat in response to the cheers.

The vision of him was so vivid in her mind that
somehow as she turned her head, instinctively and
saw him standing in the doorway she was not startled
or surprised. It just seemed inevitable!

They looked at each other for a long moment.

It was as if they found each other after an age-old
separation and were reunited.

Then the Earl said automatically, almost as if he
was thinking of something else:

"Why did you bar me out?"

"How did you . . . manage to get . . . in?"

"I followed your Nurse and she left the panel ajar."

"She would be . . . horrified if she knew you were
. . . here!"

"I want to talk to you. I *have* to talk to you!"

Demelza drew in her breath at the insistence in
his voice. As if he felt she was going to refuse his
request, he said:

"I understand if you feel it is unconventional that
we should talk here, but where else can we go?"

For a moment he realised she did not understand
what he was saying; then, as if it suddenly struck her
that the Priests'-Room was also her bed-room, the
blood rose in her cheeks and she said a little shyly:

"I . . . had not thought of it . . . before, but there is . . . nowhere. . . ."

She paused, then she added:

"I could . . . meet you in the herb-garden. I can reach . . . there without . . . anyone seeing me . . . leave the house."

"No-one knows I have returned," the Earl said, "so I will go there at once."

He looked into her eyes raised to his, and asked:

"You will come? This is not just a trick to be rid of me?"

"No . . . of course not! I will come . . . if you really . . . want me to."

"I want it more than I can possibly say. I have to talk to you."

There was a note of command in his voice and he knew that she responded to it.

"I will come!" she said simply. "But first you must return the way you came."

"Will I find the catch?"

"If you take the candle, it is quite clear from this side of the panel."

She handed him the candle as she spoke and without another word he turned and went down the stairs.

As Demelza had said, the catch, which was so invisible on one side of the door, was easy to find from the staircase.

The Earl set the candle down on one of the stairs, then went into the bed-room, closing the secret panel behind him.

There was still no-one about and he made his way down the secondary staircase and out through the door which led towards the stables. But now he turned in the opposite direction, walking past the front of the house.

In the ever-deepening dusk he found his way to the herb-garden.

He knew that Demelza would expect him to sit in the arbour, and the scent of the honeysuckle which climbed over it made him feel almost as if she were waiting for him there.

He sat down on the wooden seat, thinking that never in his life had he had a love-affair with such a strange beginning or such an intriguing one.

As he waited for Demelza he could hardly believe his own excitement.

It seemed to be rising in him. making his heart beat quickly. He might have been a boy of eighteen meeting his first love rather than a blasé cynic who had, he believed until now, tasted all the joys of love and found that they had grown tedious.

It suddenly struck him that perhaps after all Demelza would not come and never again would he be able to enter the secret passage and find his way to her room.

Then he told himself that no-one could look so pure, so honest at the same time, and, lie. If she told him she would come, then she would keep her word.

He thought it was fitting that someone so spiritual, with an aura of Holiness that he had never before found in any woman who had attracted him, should be housed in a room sanctified by those who had received Mass from an ordained Priest.

He was still alone and now he began to be afraid.

Perhaps at the last moment Demelza had thought it too much of a risk to leave her hiding-place.

Perhaps someone had seen her when she emerged from one of the doors which only she could open and no-one else had found.

Then, as his fears and apprehensions seemed to taunt him, he saw her.

She was coming towards him like the ghost he had first thought her to be, moving so silently and so effortlessly over the path between the rows of herbs that it was difficult to believe she was real.

Then at last she was beside him and as he rose to his feet she said:

"I am sorry if I kept you ... waiting. The bushes had grown so thickly round the secret door into the garden that it was difficult to get ... through."

"But you are here," he said, "and I want more than I can ever tell you, Demelza, to talk to you again."

"I wanted to tell you how glad I was that Crusader won," she answered, "but I think you would have known that."

"It was entirely due to you," he said, "and both Crusader and I are very grateful!"

"It was the most exciting race I have ever watched."

"That is what I thought," The Earl agreed. "And it was particularly exciting for me because I knew you were watching it too."

It was what Demelza herself had felt and she looked up at him. Then as if she felt shy she looked away again.

"I want to give you something to commemorate our victory," the Earl said. "But it is difficult to know what."

"No!" she replied quickly. "You must not do ... that!"

"Why not?" he asked.

"Because I would have to ... explain where the ... present had come from, and that ... as you know is ... something I ... cannot do."

The Earl was silent. Then he said:

"How long do we have to go on with this pretence? I know, Demelza, and you know too, because of the things we have done together, that we mean more to each other than if we were mere acquaintances."

He waited for her to reply, but she did not do so and he continued:

"Do you really imagine that on Saturday after the races are over, or perhaps on Sunday, I can leave the Manor and forget everything that has happened here?"

Still Demelza did not speak, and after a moment he asked:

"Will you be able to forget me, Demelza, as you know I cannot forget you?"

Now he waited and after a moment she said in a low voice:

"I shall never ... forget you ... and I shall ... pray for you."

"And you imagine that will be enough? I want to see you, I want to be with you, Demelza, and, if I am honest, I want more than my hope of Heaven to hold you in my arms and kiss you."

His voice seemed to vibrate on the air between them. Then he added:

"I cannot remember ever in my life before asking a woman if I could kiss her. But I am afraid of frightening you, afraid that you will disappear, and I will never find my White Lady again."

His voice deepened as he said:

"May I kiss you, my lovely little ghost?"

He put out his arms towards her. Demelza did not move but somehow he stopped before he touched her.

"I think ... if you kissed me," she whispered, "it would be very wonderful ... more wonderful than anything I could ... imagine ... but it would be ... wrong."

"Wrong?" the Earl asked.

He waited for an explanation and after a moment Demelza said:

"I ... heard today how you had suffered as a child ... and I have thought so ... often of how you must have suffered because of your ... m-marriage ... but ... although I would wish to do ... anything you asked of me . . . it would be wrong . . . because you belong to . . . someone else."

"Are you saying that I belong to my wife?" the Earl asked incredulously.

"You are . . . married. You took a . . . sacred vow," Demelza said in a low voice.

"A vow that no human being should be required to keep in the circumstances!" the Earl replied harshly.

"I know . . . I do understand. At the same time . . . I would feel that I was doing . . . wrong . . . and that would spoil the . . . love that . . . otherwise I could . . . give you."

The Earl was very still.

He could hardly believe what he had heard Demelza say, and yet he told himself it was what he might have expected she would think, because she was so very different from any other woman he had ever known before.

Aloud he said:

"What do you know of love? The love you might have given me if you did not think it was prohibited? Tell me!"

It was a command and Demelza clasped her hands together. Then, looking away from him across the garden, she answered:

"I have thought about . . . love, and although you may think me very . . . ignorant and foolish . . . I think it is . . . something you . . . need in your life."

"You really believe," the Earl asked, and there was no mistaking the cynicism in his voice, "that I lack love?"

Demelza made an expressive little gesture with her hands.

"I think, and again you may think it foolish of me, that there are different types of love . . . and the love you have known, which is the . . . sort the beautiful

lady who would have drugged your wine gave you, is
not the same as . . ."

Demelza's voice died away and the Earl knew she
had been about to say "as mine" but was too shy.

"Tell me about your love," he said gently, "the love
you would give a man to whom you gave your heart."

"I know," Demelza began very softly, "if I loved
someone . . . very much I would never want to . . . hurt
them. In fact I would want to protect them against any
kind of pain . . . not only in the . . . body but also in
the . . . mind."

"In fact—mother love," the Earl murmured beneath
his breath.

But he did not wish to interrupt and Demelza continued:

"There would also be my love for the . . . man I . . .
married, and . . . that love is . . . I believe . . . a part of
. . . God, who . . . created everything which is beautiful, everything which grows and is . . . part of . . . Cre-
ation."

She glanced towards him as she spoke, wondering
if he was smiling cynically at what she was trying to
describe. Then because she was nervous she went on
quickly:

"Lastly . . . I think if I was in love . . . I would want
to learn not only of . . . love but . . . everything a man
like . . . yourself could teach, because you have so
much . . . experience and inveitably you would have
. . . wider horizons than the . . . woman who . . . loved
you."

There was silence and after a moment the Earl
said:

"Would it be possible to find the love of mother,
wife, and child all in one person?"

"If it was . . . real love . . . the love that really . . .
matters . . ." Demelza replied, "then I believe it would
be possible."

She glanced at him before she went on:

"It would be like ... seeking for the ... Golden Fleece . . . the Holy Grail, and perhaps the . . . Gates of Heaven, but it would be the love that human beings were originally . . . promised in the Garden of Eden."

Her voice was very moving and the Earl drew in his breath before he said:

"And like the angel who stood with the flaming sword in that garden you are keeping me out."

He felt rather than saw the pain in her eyes, and he knew, because her fingers were linked together tensely, that he had hurt her.

"I have ... no wish to do that," she cried, "but ... how can I . . . help it?"

"How can you be so cruel? How can you deny me what you know in your heart belongs to me?"

She did not reply.

"Look at me, Demelza!"

Obediently she raised her head. The dusk had turned to night, and the moon's first rays of silver were on her face.

He looked into her troubled eyes, which held both faith and an innocence in their purple depths.

He lingered on the softness of her parted lips and he knew that where they were both concerned time had no meaning and this was what he had been seeking all his life.

He saw the questioning expression on Demelza's face alter.

Now there was a sudden radiance, as if she felt, as he did, that they had met across eternity and they were no longer separate individuals but one.

It was not only what they saw, it was there in the joining of their hearts, and deeper still in the stirring of their souls, reaching out towards what had been lost yet now had been found.

It was so beautiful, so transcendently divine, that

they were enveloped in a light which came from within themselves, more vivid than the moonlight from above.

"You love me!" the Earl said hoarsely. "You love me, my lovely little ghost, and you belong to me!"

Yet even as he thought she would melt towards him as he felt the vibrations of her reaching out towards him, she said:

"Yes, I love you! I love you in ... every way which I have tried ... inadequately ... to explain ... but after tonight I can ... never see you again."

"Can you really credit that I would allow you to walk out of my life?" he asked angrily. "Or, rather, to bar yourself away from me?"

She was silent and he continued:

"You know that what has happened to us is something so unique and perfect that I can hardly believe that it is not a figment of my imagination—a fantasy conjured up by the mystery of the Manor itself."

"There is ... nothing else I can ... do," Demelza murmured. "Nothing!"

"That is not true," the Earl said, "and I will convince you of my love for you and yours for me."

He opened his arms resolutely as he spoke, determined to break the spell which had prevented him, against his will, from touching her.

As he did so suddenly they were both aware that someone had come into the garden and was standing at the opening between the walls, looking round him.

"Gerard!" Demelza whispered beneath her breath.

"Do not move," the Earl said so that only she could hear him. "Leave this to me."

He rose without hurry from the seat, standing up to his full height, knowing that Demelza was hidden behind him.

"So there you are, My Lord!" Gerard exclaimed. "The servants told me that you had returned and they had seen you in the garden. I wondered why you had not joined us."

The Earl walked towards him.

"I was hot and a little tired of conversation after so much chatter at the Castle," he replied.

"Then if you want to be alone, I must not . . ." Gerard began.

"No, of course not! I am delighted to see you," the Earl interrupted. "Let us go back to the house together. I have been meaning to speak to you. There are two pictures in the house which, if you are in need of money, I am quite certain would fetch a very large sum in any Sale-Room."

"Do you mean that?" Gerard asked eagerly. "I did not think there was anything worth a penny in the whole place!"

"They are both in need of cleaning," the Earl replied. "I happen to be an expert on Rubens and I would not mind wagering a large sum that the picture at the top of the stairs is one of his early paintings."

"And the other?" Gerard asked.

"In the Library in a dark corner there is, I am certain, a small, authentic Perugino."

"How fantastic!"

Demelza heard the excitement in Gerard's voice as the two men moved away into the other part of the garden.

If what the Earl said was true, she thought, then Gerard could have the horses he wanted, lead the life he enjoyed, and perhaps spent a little money on renovating the Manor.

But she knew this would not alter the position between herself and the Earl.

It was true that she loved him, loved him with her whole heart, and she thought that she would regret all her life not having let him kiss her as he had wanted to do.

She could imagine nothing nearer Heaven than feeling his arms round her and his lips on hers.

But, as she had said, it would have been wrong.

She rose from the seat in the arbour and reaching up picked a pice of honeysuckle.

She would press it in her Bible, and perhaps in the years to come that would be all she would have to remember—the one moment when she had lost her heart and it no longer belonged to her.

She raised the honeysuckle to her lips.

Then she looked in the direction of the house, listening for the Earl's voice. But there was only silence, except from overhead there came the squeak of a bat.

"Good-bye . . . my hero . . . my only . . . love!" she whispered, and her voice broke on the words.

Chapter Six

"You certainly had a good Ascot, My Lord!" Gerard Langston said as the Earl tooled his horses through the traffic outside the entrance to the course.

The Earl did not reply and he went on:

"Three winners, including the Gold Cup, is as much as any race-horse owner could wish for."

There was a note of envy in his voice which made the Earl say consolingly:

"The race in which your horse took part was one of the most exciting of the meeting."

"It would hardly be described as being completely satisfactory," Gerard answered, "considering that it was a dead heat."

He paused to add:

"It means the prize money is halved—also the bets I laid on Firebird."

"You will doubtless do better next year," the Earl said.

He spoke almost automatically, as if his thoughts were elsewhere.

Although he was not aware of it, several of his friends had looked at him in surprise when, after his

121

horse in the first race had passed the winning-post a length and a half in front of the other competitors, he had seemed curiously uninterested.

It had in fact been to the Earl a day of such frustration that he had found it almost impossible to concentrate on anything that anyone was saying to him.

He had not believed that Demelza had meant what she said on Thursday night and that she really intended never to see him again.

The following day the Earl had hurried back from the races with an exciting anticipation he had never known before, being quite certain she would meet in the herb-garden after dinner.

He had therefore insisted, rather to the surprise of his guests, that they should dine early, and had skilfully arranged for everyone but himself to play cards afterwards.

This left him free to wander, with what appeared to be a casual air, into the garden.

Sitting in the arbour covered with honeysuckle, he had waited and waited until finally he realised that Demelza did not intend to join him.

It was then for the first time that he became afraid.

He was quite certain that he would find it impossible, if she was determined to keep him out, to find again a way into the secret passages, and he wondered frantically as he went to bed how he could communicate with her.

He knew that to betray either to her brother or to Nattie the fact that they had met would seem to her an act of treachery, which she would be unlikely to forgive.

And yet what alternative did he have?

On Friday he had found that the crowds made it impossible for him to distinguish any individual among them.

If Demelza wished to hide, it would be like searching for a needle in a hay-stack to discover her in the seething mob pressing round the race-track.

What was more, the number of carriages, wagons, and carts seemed to have increased since the beginning of the week.

"What can I do? What can I do?" he asked himself over and over again.

He thought that for the first time in his life not only his luck had deserted him but also his expertise where women were concerned.

Always before the Earl had found it only too easy to make assignations with any woman who caught his fancy. That one to whom he had declared his affection should actually avoid him was a new and unpleasant experience.

With any other woman he knew that he could woo her and be certain that sooner or later she would succumb, but Demelza was different.

So different, he realised now while he was driving back to the Manor, that he was worried as he had never been worried before that he might be compelled to leave and never see her again.

He had been confident when setting out that morning that the one place he would be sure to find her was in the saddling enclosure before the second race in which Firebird was running.

He had seen Abbot, spoken to the old groom, and had wished Jem, the jockey, luck.

But, looking round at those watching the horses, he could see no-one with large, pansy-coloured eyes in a small, pointed face.

Last night, when Demelza did not come to the arbour as he had expected, he had told himself harshly that he was being a fool.

How could he be sure that he had not been beguiled by the mystery of the Manor, the secret passages

as well as her ghost-like appearances, into thinking
she was lovelier and more desirable than she actually
was?

Then he knew that his doubts betrayed his own
heart and that Demelza meant more to him than any
other woman had ever done before. If he had to dedi-
cate his whole life to searching for her he would do so.

It was infuriating to know that she was so near and
yet so far, just at the top of the house but guarded by
the mystery of an impregnable fortress.

To all intents and purposes she might as well have
been in the North of Scotland or the wilds of Cornwall.

It was all the more frustrating that she was divided
from him only by the twisting steps of a secret stairway.

Finding that even the horses had become of little
importance to him, the Earl had decided to leave after the third race.

He knew only too well that, owing to the crowds,
the difficulty of clearing the course was always worse
on the last day of the race-meeting and the fourth race
could often lag on until six o'clock or later.

He had therefore said nothing to his friends but had
set off resolutely to where his Phaeton was waiting,
feeling that few people would notice his departure.

The King had not attended Ascot since Thursday,
but the Royal Box had been at the disposal of those
with whom he was closely associated and the champagne had flowed as bountifully as when His Majesty
was present.

The Earl, however, had drunk nothing since luncheon, for he had the feeling that he must keep his brain
clear so that he could solve what had begun to appear
an almost insurmountable problem.

He found his Phaeton and was about to climb into
it when Gerard Langston hailed him.

"Surely you are not leaving so soon, My Lord?"

The young man's face was flushed from celebrating the partial victory of Firebird, and it suddenly struck the Earl that Demelza would not wish her brother to indulge further.

Accordingly, with an unusual consideration he replied:

"Yes, I am leaving to avoid the crowds. Why do you not come with me?"

It was a favour that even an older, more important man would have found difficult to refuse.

It was well known that the Earl was so fastidious about his companions, and especially those who drove or rode with him, that Gerard for a moment found it hard to reply.

Finally, as the Earl climbed into his Phaeton, Gerard managed to stammer:

"I—I should be very honoured, My Lord."

The Earl hardly waited for him to swing himself into the seat beside him before he moved his horses and Jem jumped up behind.

Then they were through the iron gates and out into the road, where country bumpkins in their smocks were rubbing shoulders with sharp-faced tricksters who had come down from London.

Gerard, saluting some of his friends, who stared at him curiously as he and the Earl passed them, was silent until they had turned off the London road onto one which rounded the end of the course.

Then he glanced at the Earl and was struck by the grim expression on his face, and he wondered if anything had annoyed him.

The Earl was in fact considering how it would be possible to approach the subject of Demelza.

It seemed rather late in the day, having stayed at the Manor since Monday, to ask Langston if he had a sister.

It was equally impossible to say: "I have met your sister and would like to meet her again."

But if he said nothing, he knew, he would be expected to leave that evening as his friends were doing, or at the very latest the next morning.

Lord Chirn and Lord Ramsgill were not even returning to the Manor and had said their good-byes that morning before they left for the race-course.

The Honourable Ralph Mear was going to London and would return to the house only to pick up his luggage.

At any moment the Earl expected Gerard Langston to ask him if he too would be departing before dinner, and he did not know what answer he should give.

'I must see Demelza again—I must!' he thought to himself.

And yet he had the unmistakable feeling that even if he betrayed her trust and sent her brother to fetch her from the Priests'-Room, she might refuse to come.

'God, what can I do?' he wondered desperately, and it was in the nature of a prayer.

Suddenly he saw her saw her ahead of them, driving in an old-fashioned gig.

He recognised Nattie first, and there was no mistaking her straight back and the grey cotton gown she always wore with a white collar and cuffs. On her head was a black straw bonnet which concealed her face, but the Earl thought he would have known her anywhere.

And there was a sylph-like figure beside her.

Demelza was in white and her unfashionably small bonnet was trimmed with a wreath of white flowers.

It struck the Earl immediately that this was the opportunity for which he had been waiting. He had only to say to the young man beside him:

"Surely that is your old Nurse ahead of us? Who is the girl with her?"

Once again, the Earl thought with a sudden elation, his luck had not failed him, and the idea seemed to lift him from what had almost been the depths of despair.

It was as if the sun had suddenly come out in the darkness of night, and his fingers tightened on the reins, slowing his horses just in case the road should widen and he should be obliged to pass the gig.

Then everything happened very swiftly.

Round the corner from a side-turning hidden by a high hedge there came a chaise with two horses travelling too fast, driven by a red-faced, middle-aged man who had obviously imbibed too freely.

It was quite impossible for him to pass the gig, which was in the centre of the road at the place where he had met it.

In a desperate effort to avoid an accident he turned his horses, but one of the wheels of his phaeton locked with a wheel of the gig, which overturned.

Controlling his own animals, the Earl watched with horror as the gig tipped over onto the verge of the road and its occupant in white was thrown from it.

It all happened so quickly that there was no time to cry out a warning or even to exclaim at what had occurred.

With expert driving the Earl pulled his own horses clear of those which had been drawing the chaise at high speed, which were now rearing and plunging, suddenly checked by the locked wheels.

While the driver of the chaise started to shout and bluster, the Earl handed his reins to Gerard Langston.

"Hold them!" he said sharply.

He sprang down from the Phaeton and was running towards the gig before either Gerard or Jem was fully aware what had occurred.

Demelza had fallen from the gig over the rough

grass which edged the road and into a dry ditch on the other side of it.

As the Earl bent down and picked her up in his arms, her bonnet fell back to be caught by its ribbons under her chin.

As he looked at her little face, with her lashes dark against her white skin, he though for one terrified moment that she might be dead.

It was a fear which struck through him with the pain of a dagger. Then he saw the bruise on her forehead and knew she had only been knocked unconscious.

He was down on one knee, cradling her in his arms, when Nattie raised herself from the rough grass into which she had fallen to say:

"Miss Demelza! Oh, my dearie—what's happened to—you?"

"It is all right," the Earl said consolingly. "She must have fallen on a stone, but I do not think any bones are broken."

Nattie, with her black bonnet on one side of her grey-haired head, stood looking bewildered and, perhaps for the first time in her life, unsure of herself.

Behind her, Jem was trying to create some sort of order out of chaos.

Willing hands had appeared seemingly from nowhere to help unlock the wheels of the two vehicles. The red-faced man's groom by now had his horses under control and the ancient horse which had drawn the gig had scrambled to its feet and was quite unconcernedly cropping the grass.

The Earl lifted Demelza up in his arms and carried her towards his Phaeton. Without waiting for instructions, Nattie followed him.

Gerard, holding the Earl's horses steady with some difficulty, leant forward as they reached the Phaeton to ask anxiously:

"Is she hurt? That damned fool had no right to drive so dangerously!"

The Earl did not answer. Instead he said to Nattie: "Can you climb up behind?"

"I think so, M'Lord."

She managed to get into the seat at the back.

Holding Demelza very carefully, her face against his shoulder, the Earl took the seat previously occupied by her brother.

"She is not badly injured, is she?" Gerard asked.

The Earl did not miss the note of concern in his voice, and he answered:

"I think she is suffering from concussion. As soon as we get back to the Manor we must send for a doctor."

"I would like to tell that idiot what I think of him!" Gerard said between gritted teeth.

The Earl thought the same, but he knew the drunkard's irresponsible driving had solved his personal problem and brought to his arms the girl who had shut him out because she thought their love for each other was wrong.

Holding her in his arms as if she were a baby, he looked down at her and thought she was even more lovely in the daylight than she had been at night.

Very gently he undid the ribbons at her throat so that he could throw her bonnet onto the floor in front of them.

Then he held her close against his heart, thinking that her hair, so pale gold as to be almost silver, was the most beautiful thing he had ever seen.

"I love you!" he wanted to cry aloud, and then instinctively he tightened his arms, knowing that never again would he let her go.

Jem had cleared the road ahead, the gig had been pushed farther onto the verge, and the old horse, released from the shafts, was being led home by the boy who had been driving it.

The chaise had a buckled wheel, but there was a chance if it was driven slowly it could reach a village where doubtless there would be a wheelwright to repair it.

"You can get through now," the Earl said.

Gerard moved the horses forward, thinking that never in his life had he expected to have the opportunity of tooling such superb animals and hoping that he would not make a fool of himself in doing so.

It was only a short distance to the Manor and the Earl knew that Jem would follow them and doubtless take a short-cut through the trees which they were unable to do.

He was, however, really concerned only with Demelza, knowing that he was holding her as he had longed to do, and wishing with an intensity that surprised even himself that he could kiss her lips.

As they passed through the rusty gates he said:

"I suggest that while I carry your sister upstairs you drive immediately to Windsor Castle. You will find that His Majesty's Physician in Ordinary is staying there. Tell Sir William Knighton I sent you and ask him to come here as quickly as possible."

Gerard gave the Earl a quick glance.

"You know she is my sister?" he asked.

"I understood you had one," the Earl replied evasively.

There was a note in his voice which made Gerard say quickly:

"She is called Demelza. She was not permitted to appear when you were giving your bachelor-party."

"Of course not!" the Earl agreed.

Gerard turned the horses to draw up outside the front door.

"You really mean me to drive to Windsor?" he

asked in the tone of a child who has been offered an undreamt-of treat.

"You had better take a groom with you," the Earl replied. "I should think Jem will have reached the gates by now."

"If not, I will wait for him," Gerard said.

There was a note in his voice which would have amused the Earl had he not been so concerned with Demelza.

The footmen ran forward to help the Earl from the Phaeton, but when they would have taken Demelza from him he shook his head.

"Help Miss Nattie," he ordered, and a flunkey hurried to obey.

With Demelza in his arms the Earl walked into the hall.

"Has there been an accident, M'Lord?" the Major-Domo asked.

The Earl did not trouble to answer but waited for Nattie. When she came to his side, her eyes only for Demelza, he said:

"Show me your Mistress's room."

Without wasting words, Nattie went ahead of him up the stairs.

Following her, the Earl thought that Demelza was so light, so fragile, that she might in fact with her pale face actually be the ghost he had originally thought her to be.

He looked down at her, noting that the mark on her forehead, which must have been made by striking a stone, was deepening on her white skin, but her body was warm and very soft and he told himself fiercely that never again would he lose her.

'You are mine! Mine for all time!' he said in his heart.

* * *

If the Earl had spent a miserable Friday, so had Demelza.

She had known when she awoke early in the morning that her head ached and her eyes were swollen because she had cried herself to sleep.

It was one thing to do what was right and tell the Earl that she could never see him again—quite another to walk alone into the darkness of the secret passage.

As she moved up the twisting staircase to the Priests'-Room she knew that she was shutting herself away from the world and from the Earl in particular.

"I love him! I love him!" she cried to the Holy picture over the altar.

While she knew she was doing what was right in the eyes of God, her human body cried out for the Earl with an intensity which became more and more painful.

It was with the utmost difficulty that she prevented herself from running down the stairs to unbar the secret panel which led into her father's bed-room.

'If I could only see him once again! If I could let him kiss me good-bye,' she pleaded in her conscience, 'then I should have something to remember, something to hold close in my heart for the rest of my life.'

But she knew that if she once gave in to the impulse which made her want the Earl's arms round her and his lips on hers, it would then be impossible to deny him anything else he asked.

She had never imagined that love could be so fierce or so cruel. She felt as if she was being torn apart by her desire for a love that was forbidden.

How, she wondered, could all this have happened? And yet even with the agony she was suffering she would not have had it different.

The Earl embodied everything that she had ever

dreamt a man could be, and although she might never see him again, she knew his image would always be there not only in her heart but before her eyes.

How could there be another man to equal him? How could there ever be another man who could thrill her as he did, so that when he was beside her she became pulsatingly alive in a manner she had never known before?

"This is love!" she told herself.

Then because it was out of reach, because she had deliberately walked away from it, the tears came.

At first they only gathered in her eyes, then ran slowly down her cheeks until suddenly a tempest shook her so that she threw herself down on the bed to cry until her pillow was wet.

Later in the night she tortured herself with the idea that the Earl would easily forget her.

He had so many beautiful women in his life who would be only too ready to console him; women as lovely as Lady Sydel, and Lady Plymworth, of whom Lady Sydel had been so jealous.

It was obvious that in a few weeks, perhaps sooner, he would forget the ghost who had intrigued him for a short while.

"But I shall never forget!" Demelza said as she sobbed. "I am a ghost who has fallen in love and therefore will be haunted for the rest of my life!"

She cried until she fell asleep and her only thought to lighten the darkness was that although he could not see her, she could at least see the Earl.

"If you asks me," Nattie said when she brought Demelza's breakfast, "five days racing is too much for anybody! You looks washed out, and there's Master Gerard in a state of agitation over Firebird and asking for brandy at breakfast-time. I don't know what your mother would say to hear him—that I don't!"

She had not waited for Demelza to reply but had hurried downstairs to minister to Gerard, who had always been her favourite, while Demelza, because she did not wish Nattie to be concerned, had done her best to wash away the traces of tears.

Whatever she felt about the Earl, it was impossible not to worry about Firebird.

After all, she and Abbot had trained him, taking him round and round the course early in the mornings in all sorts of weather and often finding it difficult to obtain enough money to feed him properly.

"Sir Gerard will take all the credit if he wins," Demelza said once to Abbot, "but the glory will be ours! We have done all the hard work."

"That's true enough, Miss Demelza," Abbot had answered, "and I doubt if Master Gerard'll ever realise how much you've done to bring this 'ere horse to the peak of condition."

"Do you really think he is at his peak?" Demelza asked a week before the meeting.

"If he ain't, it's not your fault or mine, Miss Demelza," Abbot had replied. "But don't you go worryin' about him. With a bit o' luck he'll win."

Demelza remembered his words and had found them comforting as she and Nattie had set out in the gig for the races.

Today, because Abbot was with Firebird, they were being driven by a rather stupid boy who was employed in the stables because he was cheaper than any other lad would have been.

"I don't like leaving you with only Ben t' drive you tomorrow, Miss Demelza," Abbot had said when they drove back from the course on Friday evening.

"Ben will be all right," Demelza answered. "You will have too much to do with Firebird to worry about us."

"Just you tell him to stay with the gig and not go a-wandering off in the crowds," Nattie said sharply. "If he does, he's quite capable of forgetting we're there and leaving us to drive ourselves home."

"I'll see he does as he's told," Abbot promised, and Ben in fact stayed with the gig the whole day.

Because she was sure that the Earl would be looking for her, Demelza, to Nattie's surprise, had not insisted on going to the saddling enclosure before the race.

"I was sure you'd be wanting to give all sorts of last-minute instructions to Jem," she said.

"Jem is a good jockey and it is too late for words," Demelza replied.

But even as she spoke she knew that every nerve in her body was aching to go to the enclosure, not to see Jem or Firebird, but to see the Earl.

She knew how pleased he would be that one of his own horses had won the first race. At the same time, she was certain that he would be watching Firebird and perhaps wishing Gerard good luck.

It was the first time that Gerard's name had appeared on the race-card as an owner, and she longed to be beside him to share both his excitement and his pride.

'He will be very proud when Firebird wins,' she thought.

She felt a pang of anxiety in case the horse failed and Gerard was faced with large gambling debts and no money with which to settle them.

Then she remembered the thousand guineas which the Earl had paid for renting the Manor.

There were so many ways they could use it on the Manor, but she was convinced that Gerard would expend it all to easily on his life in London.

She gave a little sigh, and Nattie, hearing it, said:

"Now don't you go fretting about that horse, Miss Demelza. It'll win if it's meant to win; and if it isn't, there's nothing you can do about it."

Her words forced a faint smile to Demelza's lips.

"You are always such a comfort, Nattie dear," she said.

She thought even as she spoke that she would need all the comfort her old Nurse could give her in the future.

She saw the Earl moving about the enclosure in front of the Royal Box. She also saw him walking through the crowds towards the saddling enclosure.

Only by an exertion of will-power that was more demanding than any she had ever had to use before did she prevent herself from running across the track and going to his side when he was speaking to Abbot.

By standing up in the gig she could watch him pat Firebird's neck and say a word of encouragement to Jem.

Then, for fear he might see her and be drawn to her by her longing for him, she sat down and did not look again until the race began.

It was a disappointment that Firebird was not the winner, but The Bard ran better than expected, and at least, Demelza thought, Gerard would feel it no disgrace that his horse had done so well the first time it had been entered in a race.

Nattie had been even more elated than Demelza was.

"I suppose you're going to say, Miss Demelza, that it's been worth all the times you've come in chilled to the bone from riding in a north wind or looking like a drowned rat after exercising that animal in the pouring rain."

"Yes, it has been worth it," Demelza agreed, "and Gerard will be delighted."

She saw Nattie's eyes light up with pleasure and added:

"At least he should have made money at this meeting if he backed His Lordship's horses as well as Firebird."

"I've told him often enough he shouldn't gamble at all," Nattie said.

But she was not using her scolding voice, which both Demelza and Gerard knew so well.

When Nattie said it was time to leave after the third race, Demelza looked for the Earl. She told herself that this would be the last time she would ever see him.

She was aware, because Nattie had told her, that two of his guests would not be returning to the Manor.

They had both tipped Nattie generously and Demelza knew that when they were alone again and Ascot had relapsed, until next year, into the quiet, empty place it had been before, the money would be spent on food.

Demelza searched the Royal Box and the small enclosure in front of it for a sight of the tall, handsome figure which made her heart beat quicker every time she saw him.

But she could not see the Earl, and although she told herself it was absurd, she felt even more despondent than before.

Ben manoeuvred the gig with some difficulty away from the carriages and wagons lying four deep along the course, and they threaded their way through the booths and gambling-tents across the Heath.

When they reached the road it was crowded but less so than it would be after the last race was run and all the wagons, coaches, and carriages were moving at the same time towards Windsor and London.

It was very hot and Nattie said:

"I'll be glad of a nice cup o' tea as soon as I get home, and I expect, dearie, you'd like a drink of lemonade."

"It would certainly be cooling," Demelza answered.

"I'll put some ice in it," Nattie said. "The Chef had a large block delivered today to cool the champagne for the gentlemen. That's something we don't often see at the Manor."

Demelza was not listening.

She was thinking of the Earl standing in the Drawing-Room for perhaps the last time and remembering how handsome she had thought him when she looked at him first through the peep-hole.

Even then she had loved him, although she had not been aware of it.

In a voice that she had difficulty in making sound casual she asked:

"Is His Lordship . . . leaving this . . . afternoon?"

She never heard the answer to her question, for at that moment the horses drawing the chaise came round the side-turning, and a split second before they reached the gig, while Ben belatedly began to draw his horses to the left, Demelza knew there must be an accident.

She wanted to cry out a warning, but before she could do so there was the shuddering impact of the wheels colliding and she felt the gig tipping over.

Then there was darkness and she knew no more. . . .

* * *

She came back to consciousness moving, she thought, down a long, long tunnel towards a faint light at the far end of it.

She felt weak and somehow disembodied. It was hard to move, and yet something told her she must do so.

Then Nattie was beside her, lifting her head in the manner in which she had done ever since she was a child, holding something to her lips.

"Wh-what has . . . happened?" Demelza tried to ask, but she could not hear herself make a sound.

After a moment, as if she knew what she wanted, Nattie said:

"It's all right. You're safe!"

"There . . . was . . . an . . . accident?"

"Yes, an accident," Nattie agreed, "and you hurt your head on a stone, but the doctor says you've no bones broken and you've just suffered a little concussion."

"I . . . am . . . all right."

It was a statement, but Nattie took it as a question.

"Perfectly all right! His Majesty's own Physician came to see you—not once but twice!"

"Twice."

Demelza repeated the word, then asked:

"How long . . . ago?"

"He came first yesterday when the accident happened, then again today. He said if we wanted him he'd come down from London. A nice expense that'd be!"

Demelza must have looked concerned, because Nattie added quickly:

"No need to worry. We're not paying. His Lordship saw to all that."

"H-His . . . Lordship?"

"Yes. Very kind he was, and wouldn't leave until Sir William had seen you for the second time."

"He has . . . left?"

Nattie patted the pillows and laid Demelza's head gently down on them.

"Yes, he left this morning. There's nothing to keep him here, now that the races are over."

"No ... nothing," Demelza repeated, and shut her eyes.

* * *

Later in the afternoon Nattie insisted on Demelza eating something, and although it was difficult to do so she felt better afterwards.

"Where is Gerard?" she asked, feeling it strange that he had not come to see her.

"He went back to London with His Lordship, leaving Rollo here," Nattie answered. "And a good thing, if you asks me. That horse needs a rest."

Demelza thought how pleased Gerard would be to travel in the company of the Earl. But they had gone, and although she told herself it was foolish she felt neglected.

"Master Gerard spoke of coming back one day next week," Nattie said, "so you'd best be getting yourself well. And Abbot wants to see you. Real concerned he's been, in case it was Ben's fault the accident happened."

"You told him Ben could not help it?"

"hat boy should have been more on the left," Nattie said, as if she could not help criticising. "At the same time, the gentleman in the chaise was a-driving like a maniac! What I always says is ..."

Nattie chattered on but Demelza ceased to listen. She was thinking of the Earl and Gerard returning to London and that now the house would be very quiet.

There would be no laughter coming from the Dining-Room, and her late father's bed-room would be empty. There would be no need to bar the secret panel by the fireplace.

She thought of how she had saved the Earl from the lovely lady who had tried to drug him and how she had saved Crusader from the same fate.

Those were the ghosts, she thought, who would haunt her, and most of all, when she went to the arbour covered in honeysuckle she would think of the Earl waiting for her there.

She remembered how she had felt something live within her, thrilling and exciting, reaching out towards him so that although they had never touched each other they were very close.

She felt the tears prick her eyes. then she knew she was past crying. It was all over and the future was dull and lifeless.

*   *   *

Demelza walked down the stairs rather carefully because if she moved quickly she still felt a little dizzy. If Nattie had had her way, she would have stayed in bed.

"Why're you in such a hurry to get up?" Nattie aked in her scolding voice. "There's nothing to get up for."

That was the truth, Demelza agreed. At the same time, it was somehow worse to stay in bed, with nothing to do but think, than to move about.

She had therefore insisted, after she had eaten the luncheon that Nattie had brought her in bed, on getting up and dressing.

She put on one of her white gowns and arranged her hair, seeing as she looked in the mirror that she was very pale and her eyes seemed almost unnaturally large and dark.

"Now don't you go doing too much," Nattie was saying. "I'll be busy in the kitchen, but I'll bring you

a cup of tea at about four o'clock. Then you'll go
back to bed."

She did not wait for Demelza to reply, but bus-
tled away, intent on scrubbing and cleaning now that
the visitors had gone, even though there was no urgency for it.

Demelza reached the hall and noted that the roses
on the table at the bottom of the stairs were shedding
their petals and the bowl needed replenishing.

The flowers in the Drawing-Room were also a
little overblown but their fragrance was still in the
air, and she walked to the window wondering if she
was strong enough to reach the arbour.

Then she knew she could not face it so soon and
the intensity of the feeling it would evoke.

She would have to steel herself to become strong.
Then she could conjure up and remember the magic
that had happened there and the pulsating wonder of
the Earl's voice when he told her that he loved her.

Her memories were going to be agony to live with,
Demelza thought, but what else could she do?

She stood at the window looking out at the garden,
at the sun shining on the rhodedendrons, the beauty of
them in some way a solace for her aching heart.

She heard the door of the Drawing Room open
but did not turn her head, waiting to hear Nattie
scolding her because she was not sitting down and
putting her feet up as she had been told to do.

Then, as there was only silence, which was very unlike Nattie, she turned, and suddenly her heart seemed
to leap in her breast and it was impossible to breathe.

It was the Earl who stood there and he was looking
as overpowering, elegant, and handsome as he had
in her thoughts ever since she had regained consciousness.

She looked at him wide-eyed, thinking it could not
be true.

Only as he reached her side did she feel as if a paralysis which had held her speechless dissolved and she could tremble.

"You are better?"

His voice was deep and she felt herself vibrate to the tone of it.

"I . . . I am . . . well."

"I have been desperately worried about you."

"Why . . . why are you . . . here?"

He smiled.

"I have brought Gerard back with me and an Art Dealer. They are at the moment inspecting the pictures in the Gallery where I first saw you."

"That was . . . kind of you."

The words seemed to come fitfully through her lips.

It was so hard to speak when he was looking at her in the way he was doing now.

"Come and sit down," the Earl said. "I want to talk to you."

She looked at him enquiringly and because something about him compelled her she moved from the window to sit down on the sofa by the fireplace.

"There is a lot we have to say to each other," the Earl said, "but first—and most important of all—is, how soon will you marry me, my darling?"

Demelza looked at him in astonishment. Then, because he was waiting for an answer, she managed to stammer:

"I . . . I . . . thought . . . I . . . understood . . ."

"That is one of the things I have to explain," the Earl said, "and in a way to ask your forgiveness."

"My . . . forgiveness?"

He was sitting beside her but he rose to stand with his back to the fireplace. Then he said in a grave voice which she had not heard before:

"I have in fact deceived you, although I did not

mean it to be like that. My wife has been dead for over five years!"

Demelza's eyes were on his, but she could not speak.

She only felt as if the mists of misery which had held her were dissolving and the clouds were parting and a long, golden ray of sunshine was seeping through them.

"I am not going to tell you what I suffered," the Earl continued, "when shortly after my marriage, which had been arranged by my parents some years before it happened, my wife went mad. Suffice to say that when finally I was obliged to send her to an asylum I swore that never again would I allow myself to be humiliated in similar circumstances."

He drew in his breath as if he remembered the horrors which he had never before spoken of to anyone but which had left scars which he believed would never heal.

"But I found," the Earl went on, "when I entered the Social World alone, ostensibly as a bachelor, that not only could I forget but that my peculiar position could be turned to advantage."

He did not need to elaborate, because Demelza understood that while women found him irresistibly attractive, there was no question of having a permanent position in his life or of expecting a legal alliance.

"There is no need for me to tell you," the Earl said, "that, having discovered there was some compensation in being a married man without ties, I kept my wife's death, when it happened, a secret even from my closest friends."

He looked at Demelza as he spoke. Then he said quietly:

"I vowed that I would never marry again, and even when I met you, my darling, I had no wish to tie myself."

"I can . . . understand that," Demelza said in a low voice.

"But when you sent me away I knew that I could not live without you."

There was silence for a moment before the Earl said:

"I was determined, whatever the obstacles you put in my way, to see you, to be with you. But when I saw you thrown out of the gig in front of me, I knew that if you died I had no wish to go on living."

He spoke so quietly that for a moment the full impact of what he was saying was not clear to Demelza.

Then, as she understood, she moved for the first time since he had been speaking and clasped her hands together tightly.

"That is why I have come back," the Earl said, "to explain what I should have explained before, and to ask you to be my wife."

Their eyes met but he did not move towards her. Instead, they looked at each other for a long time.

Then, even as he had done, Demelza rose to her feet to walk not towards him but to the window.

She stood for a moment looking out, then she said:

"I love . . . you! I love you so much that I could not . . . bear you ever to have any . . . regrets."

The Earl's eyes were on her face but he did not speak, and after a moment she said hesitatingly, as if she was feeling for words:

"Now that you are free . . . now it would not be . . . wrong from . . . God's point of view . . . and there would be . . . no-one to disapprove . . . except Gerard and Nattie . . . . I will do anything you . . . ask of me . . . but you need not make me . . . your wife."

Her voice died away and now for the first time since she had risen she turned to look at him.

She saw an expression on his face which for a moment she did not understand, then he walked towards her and took her very gently in his arms.

Her head fell back against his shoulder and he looked down at her with a tenderness which seemed for the moment to change him so completely that he might have been a stranger.

His voice was very deep and moved as he said:

"Do you really think that is what I want, my precious, my darling, my adorable little ghost? I want you as my wife. I want you because you already belong to me, because we are part of each other, and never again will I lose you."

He held her a little close before he said:

"I intend to tie you to me by every chain and vow that exists, but I believe actually we are bound to each other already and no Marriage Lines could make us any closer."

She raised her head and he saw by the sudden radiance in her eyes that this was what she wanted to hear.

For a long moment they looked at each other, then the Earl's lips sought hers.

It seemed to Demelza as if everything she had longed for was there in his kiss. At the touch of his lips the pain she had suffered vanished and instead there was a wonder and a glory which came from Heaven itself.

This was what she knew love would be like—the love of God, which was so perfect, so divine, that it was not of this world.

And yet, the closeness of the Earl and the demand which she knew lay behind the gentleness of his kiss made her feel as if her whole being was invaded by a splendour that was blinding in its intensity, and so it was so insistently marvellous that it was almost a physical pain.

She felt the pressure of his lips increase, his arms

tightened, and then he was kissing her more passionately, more masterfully, more possessively.

"I love . . . you!" she wanted to cry.

But there were no words in which to express the
fact that they had found each other and now, as they
had been since the beginning, they were not two people but one.

Chapter Seven

The sun, which had been shining warmly all day, was suddenly eclipsed by clouds which brought a scud of rain.

It was not a cold rain but warm, and almost like a drink for the thirsty earth, which had been baked dry all through the summer.

The Earl, driving his team of horses, did not slacken their pace and they moved swiftly along the narrow country roads which twisted towards the sea.

There was a hill rising slowly from a verdant valley and when they reached its summit the Earl could look down and see the vivid blue of the Atlantic and below him nestling amongst the trees the chimneys and roofs of a long, low-built house.

It was then for the first time that he pressed his horses with urgency, and there was an expression on his face which gave him a look of almost youthful eagerness.

There was still some way to go before finally he reached the house and saw it in front of him, its gardens still vivid with the colours of autumn.

Originally built as a Priory, Trevarnon House,

which had been in the Earl's family for over five hundred years, was not only beautiful but had a mellow warmth about it which made everyone who approached it seem welcome.

The rain had ceased as unexpectedly as it had begun, and now the sun was brilliant again and shone on the many-paned windows, turning them to glittering gold as if they were lit from the inside.

The Earl drew his team, sweating a little with the speed at which they had travelled, to a standstill in front of the porticoed front door.

As grooms came running from the stables he threw down the reigns and walked into the hall.

There was only an ancient Butler and a young footman in attendance, who took his hat and gloves. Then, as he would have moved past them, Dawson appeared and said:

"Her Ladyship asked me to see that you changed your coat, M'Lord, for what you're wearing'll be damp."

"There was very little rain," the Earl replied.

But Dawson stood waiting, and impatiently the Earl pulled off his tight-fitting grey whip-cord riding-coat and unbuttoned the waist-coat beneath it.

Dawson took them from him and helped him into a slightly more comfortable coat that he usually wore at home. Then the Earl saw that the valet also held in his hand a fresh muslin cravat.

"Really, Dawson," he exclaimed, "this is quite unnecessary!"

"Her Ladyship's afraid you might get a stiff neck, M'Lord."

"Have you ever known me to have such a thing?" the Earl asked.

"There's always a first time, M'Lord."

The Earl pulled his cravat from his neck and as he

took the crisp muslin which Dawson held out to him he said:

"I have a suspicion, Dawson, that I am being simultaneously mollycoddled and bullied!"

The valet grinned.

"Yes, M'Lord, but we wouldn't wish Her Ladyship to worry."

The Earl smiled.

"No, Dawson, we would not wish her to worry."

He tied his fresh cravat with skilful fingers, then walked away from the hall and down the long corridor off which opened the gracious rooms filled with family treasures which, until they came to Cornwall, he had not seen for many years.

He knew that Demelza would be in the Orangery, which had been converted by his grandfather in his old age into a Sitting-Room that was half a Conservatory and half a look-out over the gardens.

It always seemed to be filled with sunshine and now as he opened the door the fragrance of the flowers hit him almost like a wave from the sea.

There were not only the ancient orange trees which had been brought from Spain two centuries ago, there were also orchids, exotic lilies, flowering cactuses and small dwarf azaleas which had once flowered in the foothills of the Himalayas.

At the far end of the room, reclining on a *chaise-longue* by a window, was Demelza.

She had not heard the Earl's approach, and he saw in profile her face tilted upwards, her eyes raised to the skies, as if she was praying as she had been when he first saw her in the Priests'-Room.

Two brown and white spaniels who were beside her couch heard him first and as they sprang towards him Demelza rose too and it seemed as if her eyes held the sunshine in their violet depths.

"Valient! You are back!"

It was a cry of sheer joy. She ran across the room
and the Earl put his arms round her to hold her
against him.

"You are . . all right? You are . . . safe?" she questioned, but the words did not seem to matter.

It was the expression on her face that held his attention and the knowledge that because they were
touching each other nothing else was of any consequence.

"You have missed me?"

His voice was deep.

"It has been a very . . . very . . . long day."

"That is what I found."

"I was afraid the . . . rain would slow you down.
Did you get . . . wet?"

"There was only a little rain," he answered, "and,
as you see, I have changed."

"That is what I . . . wanted you to . . . do."

"You are making me soft," he complained.

She laughed gently.

"Nothing could do that, but even for someone as
. . . strong as . . . you, there is no point in taking . . .
risks."

As she spoke she slipped her hands under his coat,
saying:

"Your shirt is not damp?"

His arms tightened as he felt her hands on his
back, caressing the strong, athletic muscles beneath
the soft linen, and there was a touch of fire in his
eyes.

He bent his head and found her lips and they were
locked in a kiss which swept away every thought except that they were together.

The kiss lasted a long time, and when finally the
Earl released Demelza her face was radiant and her
lips soft and parted from the insistence of his.

"Darling, I have . . . so much to . . . tell you," she

said in a voice that trembled a little, "but first you must have something to eat and drink. You have been on the road for a long time."

She took him by the hand and pulled him to where at the side of the Orangery there was a table on which there were several covered silver dishes, heated underneath by lighted candles.

There was also a wine-cooler filled with ice, in which repcsed an open bottle of champagne.

"Cornish pasties made just as you like them," Demelza said, "and crabs that were caught this morning in the bay."

"I am hungry," the Earl admitted, "but I do not wish to spoil my dinner."

"There is still two hours before we dine," she replied. "I made it late in case you were delayed."

The Earl took a Cornish pasty from the silver dish and poured himself out a glass of champagne.

Then, with his eyes on his wife, he sat down in a comfortable chair while she resumed her position on the wide *chaise-longue* which was covered with satin cushions.

"Now, tell me what you have done," she said eagerly.

"I bought two exceptional mares in Penzance," the Earl replied, "which I am sure will improve our stock and should be just the right age for Crusader when we put him to stud, after he has won the Derby."

"You are very confident of doing that?" Demelza teased.

"How could I think otherwise when he is your horse and mine?" the Earl answered.

"I am glad that your journey was so . . . fruitful," she said. "I was afraid you might have gone all that way only to be . . . disappointed."

"I knew Cardew had some good horses," the Earl replied, "but these are exceptional."

"I also have some . . . news for . . . you," Demelza said.

The Earl waited, his eyes on her face, one hand absent-mindedly caressing the ear of one of the spaniels, which was trying to gain his attention.

"The jumps were finished today."

It was obviously an announcement of some significance.

"Finished?" the Earl exclaimed. "Did Dawson tell you that?"

"He wanted to surprise you," Demelza said, "and so did I. They are exactly the same as those that are erected on the Grand National Course."

She paused to add:

"You now have a chance of winning both the Grand National and the Derby."

"It is certainly a challenge," the Earl said, "but I am new to steeplechasing and it may prove more difficult than training Crusader for the flat."

"It will give you another interest."

He glanced at her sharply before he asked:

"Are you suggesting I need one?"

She looked at him in a way which expressed more clearly than words her inner feelings.

"I am always . . . afraid," she said softly, "that you will begin to be . . . bored, without parties . . . without all the amusing, witty . . . people who have always . . . surrounded you."

The Earl smiled as if something secretly amused him, then he said:

"Do you really think I would miss them when I have something here with you that I have never before had in my whole life?"

He saw the question in Demelza's eyes, but before she could ask it he said:

"A home! That is what all my money has never

been able to buy. The home I did not have as a child
but which I have found here."

"Oh, Valient, is that . . . true? It is what I have
prayed I might give you."

The Earl put down his glass of champagne and rose
to his feet to stand at the window looking at the
exquisite view which ended in a distant horizon.

"London seems very far away," he said after a
moment's silence.

"People will soon be . . . returning . . . there for the
winter . . . season."

"Are you tempting me?" The Earl asked, and there
was a hint of amusement in his voice.

"It is something I have no . . . wish to do," Demelza
answered. "You know that for me, being here with
you is like . . . being in Heaven. I have never been so
happy."

He walked towards her and sat down on the edge of
the *chaise-longue,* facing her.

"Have I really made you happy?" he asked.

He knew the answer before she said, with a depth
of intensity in her voice that was very moving:

"Every day I think it is impossible to be happier or
to love you more. Then every . . . night I find I was
mistaken, and you give me an . . . ecstatic new love
which I did not know . . . existed."

The Earl did not reply but just sat looking at her,
and after a moment she asked a little anxiously:

"What are you . . . thinking?"

"I am wondering what it is about you that holds me
spellbound every time I see you. I think really you are
not a ghost but a witch."

Demelza laughed.

"I am certainly no longer a ghost," she said. "I am
the one who is . . . haunted, as I have been ever since
the first . . . moment I saw . . . you."

"Do you suppose I am not haunted too?" the Earl

asked in a deep voice. "Haunted not only by your eyes, your lips, and your exquisite body, my darling, but by your heart, and most of all by your love. That is something from which I wish never to escape."

"Would you . . . want to?" Demelza asked.

"Do you expect me to answer such a foolish question?" he enquired. "If you are happy, how do you suppose I feel, knowing you are mine, knowing we have everything in the world that really matters!"

"Oh, Valient!"

Demelza put out her arms towards him, but he still sat, looking down at her, searching her face as if it was so precious, so perfect, that he must commit every line of it to his memory.

"I have something else to tell you," she said. "I received a letter today from Gerard."

"I expected you would hear from him soon."

"He is so thrilled that you have allowed him to keep his new race-horses in your stables at Newmarket. That was very . . . kind."

"There was plenty of room," the Earl replied carelessly, "now that we have so many of those that matter here."

"And Gerard feels so well off now that he has obtained so much money from the sale of the paintings, which only you recognised as being valuable."

She looked at the Earl from under her eye-lashes as she went on:

"I think, if you are truthful, you . . . forced the Art Dealer into paying more money for them than he would . . . otherwise have . . . done."

"I certainly made him pay what I considered was their true value, and refused to allow him to treat Gerard as a greenhorn as regards Art, which actually he is."

"It has made him very happy," Demelza said with a smile.

"I am more concerned with the feelings of his sister," the Earl replied.

"Do you want me to tell you how . . . grateful I am?"

"I like it when you are grateful," the Earl said, "but my interest in your brother was really entirely selfish. I do not wish you to worry about him, but only about me."

Demelza laughed.

"You are very . . . possessive."

"Not only possessive," the Earl replied, "but fanatically jealous. I cannot bear, and this is the truth, Demelza, that you should think of anyone or anything except myself. I want to possess every particle of you."

His voice deepened as he went on passionately:

"I want to possess you as a woman. I want you to be mine from the top of your head to the soles of your tiny feet, but I want too your mind, your heart, and your soul."

His lips touched her cheek.

"I warn you, my darling, as I have warned you before, that I am jealous even of the air you breathe!"

"Oh, Valient, you know already that I . . . belong to you in every . . . possible way. I am part of you and I know that if you . . . died or grew . . . tired of me I should really become the ghost you once . . . thought me to be."

"That I should grow tired of you is a possibility we need not even contemplate," the Earl said, "and I intend, God willing, that we should both live until we are very old."

"It can never be long enough for me," Demelza murmured, "but you must try, my darling husband, not to be too . . . jealous."

"Why should I try to be anything but what I am?" the Earl asked. "Jealousy is a new emotion where I am concerned, and although I find it painful, there are compensations in knowing that I must fight and strive to possess you as completely as I wish to do."

"Fight?" she questioned.

"Sometimes I feel that there is something elusive about you," the Earl answered, "some secret within you that is not wholly mine."

"Why . . . should you . . . think that?"

Now her eyes were veiled and her lashes were dark against the translucence of her white skin.

"There is something," the Earl said almost as if he spoke to himself. "At night when you are lying in my arms after we have touched the wings of ecstasy, I feel that we are so close, so completely one, that our hearts beat in unison and we have no life apart from each other. Then, when the day comes—"

"What . . . happens . . . then?"

"I feel you have escaped me," the Earl replied, "just as I feel now there is something—but what it can be I have no idea—that you are hiding."

He reached out suddenly and put his hands on her shoulders.

"What is it?" he questioned. "What are you withholding from someone who would possess you utterly —the man who worships you, but at the same time is your conqueror?"

Demelza was very soft and yielding beneath the grip of his hands and the almost violent note in his voice.

"Perhaps it is . . . because we are so . . . close, my darling," she said after a moment, "that we know not only every . . . inflection in the other's voice, but also every secret . . . every stirring of our . . . souls, which are so linked that we think with a . . . single thought."

"You have not answered my question," the Earl said. "You have a secret! I know it! I know it instinctively! I felt last night that there was something, and when I came into this room today I was sure of it!"

The grip of his hands tightened.

"You will not keep me in ignorance!" he stormed. "Tell me what I do not know—for I will not allow you to play with me."

"I am not ... playing with you, my beloved husband," Demelza answered. "It is only that I am ... afraid."

"Of me?"

She shook her head.

"I could never be ... afraid of you ... but perhaps a ... little of your ... jealousy."

There was a frown between the Earl's eyes.

"What could you do that would make me jealous?"

Demelza did not answer and after a pause he said:

"What are you trying to tell me?"

Demelza glanced at him, then looked away again, and he saw the faint colour rising up her face.

"Only," she said in a whisper, "that perhaps I will not be ... able to ... watch you ... win the Grand National."

For a moment the Earl did not understand, then as he took his hands from her shoulders he asked:

"Are you saying, my darling one—is it possible—so soon?"

"It is ... soon," Demelza whispered, "but, like you, I am ... sure it is a ... certainty!"

The Earl put his arms round her and held her close.

"Why did you not tell me?"

"I wanted to be ... sure."

"And you were also afraid that I might be jealous?"

"After ... what you have ... just said ... very afraid!"

"I shall be jealous if you love our children more than you love me," he said. "But I know one thing—

they will never suffer as I did from neglect and indifference, or from lack of love."

"They will never do that," Demelza agreed. "And, my wonderful...marvellous husband...we must both give them love, but you will always be first...a very easy first...you know...that."

There was a throb of passion in her voice, which brought the fire back into the Earl's eyes, but as if to hold his desires within bounds he said jokingly:

"Is it possible for a ghost to have a baby?"

"I am not a ghost," Demelza protested. "You have made me a woman...a woman who loves you so... much and so...overwhelmingly that she can imagine nothing more...perfect than to have a tiny replica of ...you."

"If I am going to give you a son," the Earl said, "I must insist on a daughter as well, who will look like you, my darling, and whom I too can love."

"The house is big enough for any number of... children," Demelza answered, "and the garden is so lovely and the sea is so near...but perhaps...."

She stopped suddenly, and the Earl, who was touching the softness of her cheek with his lips, raised his head to ask:

"Perhaps what?"

"Perhaps by the time they are ... old enough to enjoy such...things, you will want to leave Cornwall for one of your other...houses."

He smiled at her.

"I know exactly what you are doing, my precious. You are trying to safe-guard yourself against being hurt, by thinking you must not count too much on my constancy."

He saw by the flicker in Demelza's eyes that he had guessed the truth, and after a moment he said:

"Do you want me to swear that we will stay here for the rest of our lives?"

"No, of course not!" she cried. "You know that from the moment you asked me to be your ... wife, I have tried to ... leave you free. I do not want to constrain and confine you as other ... women have wished to do. I want you always to do ... exactly what you ... wish."

The Earl did not speak and after a moment she said a little shyly:

"This is what I believe real love is. To give, not to demand; to ask not for promises or reassurances except for ... those which ... come spontaneously from ... the heart."

She looked at him before she added:

"Wherever you ... go, as long as you ... take me with ... you I shall be happy and content. I do not wish you to feel tied to any ... place that might become a ... burden or an ... encumbrance. All I want is your ... happiness."

The Earl's expression was very tender.

Even after being married to Demelza for three months she could still surprise him by the depth of her feelings and by an intuition that was so attuned to his that she always said the right thing.

Was there any other woman in the world, he wondered, who would not seek to hold on to him and bind him, to make him in some way her prisoner?

He knew that because Demelza left him free he was utterly and completely her captive. Everything she said and everything she did made him want her all the more.

She was what he had sought in his imagination and never found; she was in fact what he had believed to be impossible—mother, wife, and child in one small, ethereal person.

Only occasionally did he protest at the way she cosseted him and cared for him, for he knew it was what he had always missed in his own mother.

As a wife she gave him everything that a woman deeply in love could give, and so much more besides.

He found her innocence so exciting, so fascinating, that when he taught her about love she aroused him spiritually as well as physically, as no other woman had ever been able to do.

He thought that although he would be a little jealous of his children because they would command much of her attention, he would be proud of them in the same way that he was proud of his horses and his other possessions.

But they would mean more and be more absorbing because they were an actual part of himself and of her.

In loving Demelza so wholeheartedly and in fighting to own her completely, as he had said himself, in body, mind, and soul, he had not until now given any thought to the fact that their union would result in children.

Now he knew it would complete her as a woman; a woman he would love in an even deeper and perhaps more passionate manner than he had loved the innocent and elusive girl.

Demelza was watching him with just a touch of anxiety in her eyes.

"You are ... pleased? You are ... really pleased, Valient, that we are to have ... a baby?"

"I am pleased, my precious one," the Earl answered, "but you must take great care of yourself. I will not have anyone, not even my own child, upsetting you or forcing you to take any risks."

"You must not ... mollycoddle me!"

"That is what I say to you, but you never listen."

"All I want is for ... you to love ... me," Demelza said, "even when I am not as ... pretty as you think me ... now."

"You will always be the most beautiful person I have ever seen," the Earl said positively.

He thought as he spoke that there was nothing more beautiful than a rose in full bloom.

But Demelza did not smell of roses but of honeysuckle, and he knew that because the fragrance was always with him it was impossible for him not to think of her every moment, even when they were apart as they had been today.

She knew he was waiting to say more and now he rose to pull off his coat. He threw it on the floor and sat beside Demelza on the chaise-longue, putting up his legs in his shining Hessian boots and pulling her against him.

She laid her head on his shoulder and put her arm round him to feel with her long, sensitive fingers the muscles in his back as she had done before.

"Have you any more surprises for me?" he asked, his mouth on her hair.

"I think it is ... enough for one day," she answered, "except that I want to ... tell you that I ... love you!"

"That is strange," the Earl remarked, "because it is exactly what I was going to say to you!"

He felt her lips kiss him through the soft lawn shirt and the little quiver that went through her.

The fire within flamed as he asked:

"What are you feeling, my darling?"

"Very ... thrilled ... and excited ... because I am close to you."

He put his hand under her chin and turned her face up to his.

The love in her eyes and the invitation on her lips made him turn round until, as her head sank against the soft cushions, he was looking down at her while their bodies were very close.

"There has not been a moment today when I have

not been thinking of you," he said, "and yet, in some strange way, you were with me."

"I feel ... that too," Demelza said, "but I ... wanted you! I wanted you ... desperately ... as you are ... now."

His hand moved over the curved line of her hip, then rose towards the softness of her breasts.

"You tell me I am free, my lively one," he said, "but I could never be free, even if I wished to be."

With the little gesture he loved, she raised her mouth.

Just for a moment he hesitated, as if he had more to say, and then words were unnecessary.

His lips came down on hers and he knew that beneath the softness of them there was a leaping flame which echoed the burning sensation within himself.

His heart was frantically beating against Demelza's as he drew her closer and still closer.

Then there was the fragrance of honeysuckle and the haunting mystery and inescapable wonder of love, which was as free as the wind, as deep as the ocean, and as high as the sky.

ABOUT THE AUTHOR

BARBARA CARTLAND, the celebrated romantic novelist, historian, playwright, lecturer, political speaker, and television personality, has now written over two hundred books. She has had a number of historical books published and several biographical ones, including a biography of her brother, Major Ronald Cartland, who was the first Member of Parliment to be killed in the war. The book has a preface by Sir Winston Churchill.

In private life Barbara Cartland is a Dame of Grace of St. John of Jerusalem and one of the first women, after a thousand years, to be admitted to the Chapter General.

She has fought for better conditions and salaries for midwives and nurses, and, as President of the Hertfordshire Branch of the Royal College of Midwives, she has been invested with the first Badge of Office ever given in Great Britain, which was subscribed to by the midwives themselves.

Barbara Cartland has also championed the cause of old people and founded the first Romany Gypsy Camp in the world. It was christened "Barbaraville" by the gypsies.

Barbara Cartland is deeply interested in Vitamin Therapy and is President of the National Association for Health.